The Third Wish

Deby Adair

The Unicorns of Wish Books

③

UnicornKisses

Australia

Faithfully dedicated to all creatures that fly

With sincere love and gratitude to all my 'little unicorns.'
Immeasurably - for Legs - my own faithful Pud.

Cataloguing-in-Publication is held at the National Library of Australia

Adair, Deby
The Third Wish
Revised ed.
ISBN: 978-0-9804513-2-0

First ed. published in 2011
Published in USA 2012
Revised ed. published by UnicornKisses 2019

Child and Youth Fiction

The Unicorns of Wish Books
③

Cover and Design by UnicornKisses Australia

Join us with other Kindred Spirits
www.unicornkisses.com

Contents

◆◆◆

The Legend

Rising from the mists of sunset and reaching into dawn's surprise, there is a land called Wish. Guarded by ponds and watched by noble keepers, Wish awaits and prepares for adventures.

One day, a warrior dressed in splendid clothes, and handsome as he was rich, charged the shores of Wish. His desire was to slay a unicorn. He wanted the golden horn for its hidden powers and wisdom.

No matter how much he was told that a dead unicorn's horn was of no use to anyone, he would not listen and would not be told. He wasn't wanted in Wish and was heartily ignored, but the warrior returned again and again; he would not be swayed. It was his wish and his desire to have the horn of a unicorn. He promised a huge reward to those in the land.

But what did they care for bullion or gold? Would it make them strong? Give them wisdom? Teach them to be brave, kind, or fair?

There lived a sorcerer in Wish, and he too ignored the warrior's plea, but then one sad and foreboding night the sorcerer came forward with a changed mind. And so it was. The sorcerer told the warrior where he could find a unicorn and having done his duty he asked to have his gold, but the warrior was well studied and he knew the ancient lore… mighty unicorns would not appear for just anyone, so he ordered the sorcerer to bring a unicorn to him.

The sorcerer could have taken the gold and sent the warrior home; instead, using wild magic, he changed his appearance and shape to become the image of an innocent maiden.

He sat and waited when all his trickery was complete, on a boulder of a path well used. He held his breath and waited for a sacred unicorn. Meanwhile the warrior hid in bushes nearby, with his arrows and crossbow held ready, his handsome face excited and aglow!

Soon it happened. The wait was neither long nor hard before a pure white unicorn, with shy, soft steps, made herself known. Her breathtaking golden horn shone brightly as her gossamer mane and tail flowed in all their glory to the ground. With innocent eyes open and wide, the unicorn spoke like this: 'With your once kind heart now turned cold, would you sell your soul and kill virtue, for gold? You are not a maiden, so I offer you a chance: withdraw, send the warrior away and save yourself while you can.'

Discovered in his deception, the sorcerer was not humbled. He did not bow his head or beg forgiveness. Furiously he cast away his disguise, and with a twisted face, he cried out to the warrior.

Triumphant, the warrior shot the arrow from his bow with an aim that would surely make its mark, but the unicorn swiftly turned, so her shoulder was pierced and not her heart. She screamed, though, and to hear a unicorn scream is to hear the end of all that is fair.

The sound of her torment was heart-rending, desolate, a thing of dire anguish, and so it was that in that moment, the *warrior knew what he had done. With blinding clarity he threw down his arrows and flung away his cruel crossbow, then ran in dread to fall at her feet.*

'Forgive me,' he sobbed, 'please forgive my black-hearted soul!'

Although pain throbbed in her sacred horn, and in agony her innocent shoulder bled, the unicorn knew the need for pity and this is what she said: 'Warrior, save yourself while you can. This was your wish, so now, to save your lost soul, you must wish for something to heal my wound.'

The warrior had been unthinking in his deeds; he had craved power and done anything to satisfy the means. Now, with true remorse, he wished to heal her at any price and in the very instant of his wishing he lost his human form to become a small tree with dark green leaves that were trimmed in brightest gold. The unicorn ate several leaves then sure enough, the torn, blood-drenched hole closed over, as if it had never been!

Angered, the sorcerer cursed aloud. He must either run in fear or deal with the living unicorn. With sadness in her velvet eyes, the unicorn turned to him and spoke: 'You are an outcast. You are ugly, damaged, and very, very sad. You have my pity, so I too make a wish and this is what I say: 'Let the gold the warrior paid you, forever disappear. And may you be shunned by all until the day you make amends.'

The riches that the warrior had bestowed vanished, and were never seen again, and so it was that the sorcerer knew defeat, and he cursed with anguish and angry tears.

The unicorn had fulfilled her task. She knew there was nothing left to do, so with the speed of birds and the legs of horse, she galloped away, far away.

For a while, Wish was quiet again.

I ask a question
This I ask of you…
Is doing right
Even if your heart should break
A greater thing than being happy
Whichever means that might take?

I ask a question
This I ask of you…
Does a cheerful coward
Have greater worth
Than a hero
Who is sad but true?

I ask a question
This I ask of you…
How are we judged
At the last…
Is it by the length of life
Or what we do from end to start?

CHAPTER 1

Phantom in the mist

Rielle lay stunned by the fall she had just taken. Above her, on the lee of the cliff, Pud whined then scrambled to reach his mistress. Fog lingered above Rielle's face, drifting with fingers coated in a soft and slimy jelly. Rielle gasped. She was hurt; hurt badly. She tried to raise her head. *Where is everyone?* Then she heard the snarl. With an effort that made sweat bead her brow and caused her star-scar to hurt, she looked up.

The wolf had her cornered. Staring with red-rimmed eyes, it raised its lip in a blood-chilling growl, slowly and with utmost precision. Rielle watched, fascinated, as if she wasn't there, as if she were not the one being hunted. With delicious purpose, the wolf tiptoed toward her. Placing each foot down as if gliding on egg shells, it crept forward in the eternal ballet of the hunter.

Rielle could see each and every one of its teeth become gleaming objects layered in savage tendrils of saliva. *Where is everyone?* With blissful release, she fainted.

The wolf hesitated, raised its head and sniffed. Warily, it placed all four feet on the ground and looked back.

Pud stood there like a dark, shiny herald from another world. In the misty light, his huge black body towered over the mottle-coated wolf. Pud edged forward, a growl strangling from him in a resonating pitch that filled the mountainside with strains of fearful eagerness.

The wolf blinked. Forgetting Rielle, it turned to face its opponent.

Having distracted the stalker from his beloved mistress, Pud raised his head and howled with urgent desolation. In a swift movement that stunned the mottle-coated wolf, two huge grey wolves appeared by Pud, poised ready for the fight. Briefly, the mottle-coated wolf looked confused, then, grinning with ferocity, it turned tail and ran. Pud and the grey wolves did not follow.

The mottle-coated wolf scurried away and, impossibly, it began to laugh - a human sound. As the fog covered its passing, it paused fleetingly, glaring back at Rielle and her protectors with livid eyes, before disappearing into the ragged darkness.

Pud ran to his mistress. Rielle was blue-lipped and breathing so shallowly that she might already have reached the end.

Immediately, with a whispered word, Enin On, Number Nine of the First Ones, or Hope as he was called in Wish, changed from grey wolf to be himself again. Holding the *Wand of Faith* to Rielle's failing heart, Hope channelled beams of blue light into her motionless body.

Swiftly, Oobaat the gatekeeper, Eno On, Number One of the First Ones, also resumed human shape. Placing the *Staff of Life* against Rielle's mortal wound, he streamed light to dance around her, like a joyful wraith in the murky fog.

With a gasp that made her frail body lurch, Rielle jolted forward and sat up, coughing. The blood soaking her tunic stopped flowing and her eyes took on the look of the living again.

Fiercely, Rielle grasped Oobaat's arm. A familiar expression lit her face, almost as if she hoped he were someone else. Taking another deep breath, she looked away. Tears dripped down her cheeks as she flung herself against Oobaat, sobbing.

'There, there, little one,' Oobaat soothed, as Hope shook his head at her troubled sadness. 'We hadn't left you; we just got sidetracked. But you're well again now. You're alive.' Oobaat's heart went out to her. She was a brave girl; there was no doubt about that.

'Where is everyone?' Rielle whispered weakly, as Hope kneeled down to check on her once more.

Pud nudged his way forward before Hope could answer, then licked Rielle's ear and placed his paw gently onto her shoe.

'At this very moment, the entire unicorn herd is searching for Will,' Hope breathed, his eyes flickering at the mist around them, 'except Benny who is here with us.'

Silently, the unicorn appeared from a hidden pocket of mist. Rielle brightened at the sight of him.

'Will too, is lost in the fog,' Benny whispered, nodding kindly at her, 'and we don't sense him anywhere.'

Rielle frowned. 'He should be alright,' she questioned, 'surely? After all, he has the *Wand of Time* for protection.'

She rushed the last sentence, peering urgently at the First Ones.

Hope and Oobaat glanced fleetingly at each other with grim expressions. Watching them, Rielle knew their disappointment.

It had been too long and too hard a climb up the mountain, burdened with battles and cruel uncertainties that had taken a toll on all of them.

'Will refuses to use the wand,' Oobaat muttered, 'yet he carries her around like a trophy.' His eyes flashed. 'He will not learn to control her, no matter how urgent the need or how much we plead with him to do so.'

Rielle sighed and nodded. The fog was lifting; hopefully the unicorns would find Will soon. She held a hand to the spot where her wound had been. It was sticky and wet. She grimaced in disgust.

'Thank you,' she said to the First Ones, 'thank you for saving my life.'

'Thank your faithful dog,' Oobaat replied pensively.

'Thank Benny, too,' Hope cut in. 'He was hot on your trail. Even before we heard Pud howl, he sent us an urgent warning.'

'Well, thank you for *healing* my wound,' Rielle insisted quietly, as she hugged Pud in gratitude and held a hand out to Benny.

Oobaat nodded, unhappily. 'Yes,' he sighed, with a tired frown, 'it seems the wands have little time for singing these days and spend their time in healing, instead.'

...

Ever since Old had been killed in the battle of the almond orchard by the Sorcerer of Great Contempt, there had been little joy for any of them. As they had left the Valley of Possibility and journeyed on out of Wish to find Old's caves, the sorcerer had used many means to hinder and torment them and destroy their protection. Although he was still exiled in Wish, it seemed he could rule the wind and the beasts of the outside world with his powers and resolve. Just like the wolf that they could not be sure was real, at the end of each attack, the sorcerer's phantom would briefly appear before vanishing.

...

Below the high ridge the group sat upon, the sun abruptly reached out toward morning, bathing the valley beneath them in a sweet wisp of gossamer violet. With a gust at the small group by the cliff edge, the fog evaporated as if it had been nothing but their imagination.

CHAPTER 2

Sorry for me... sorry for you... Sorry for the things I do

Will heard the unicorns searching for him. He clutched the *Wand of Time* tightly, as if she, and she alone, could protect him. He wished that everyone would go away and leave him be. It had not been his idea to climb the mountain to Old's caves. All he had ever wanted was to leave Wish, but Old had given him the Wand of Time, and Will must finish what it was he'd started; he knew that, yet resentment flared inside him like a flame. Not at Old, of course, but at the way things had turned out.

He hadn't asked for any of this! Will just wanted to forget the past and to return home. He thought back to the battle in the almond orchard and winced. The memory would scorch his heart and thoughts for the remainder of his days, just as it haunted him with a clarity that would not let him sleep. As had become his habit, he pulled a small carving of an eagle from his pocket and smoothed the surface.

He sighed. He did his best to remember what home had been like, but it escaped him. Feeling foolish, he looked around for a distraction. Finding none, he laid the Wand of Time across his knees and, for a fleeting moment, was tempted to polish her golden wood. He stopped himself. If he made a start, then he would have to learn to use her power, and at the thought, the old fear clutched the pit of his stomach.

He did not feel worthy. The fear clenched him, even after Will pretended it was gone. Will had become good at pretending. With an iron grip, the fear settled to wait.

For the thousandth time, Will wished Old had not given him the precious wand, and for the thousandth time, his heart swelled with amazement at the honour. In a familiar gesture, he held her close to his cheek as thoughts fought and clashed inside him and became more confused by the kindness everyone always showed him, despite his anger and self loathing.

Will looked up, stifling a gasp. Coraggio stood beside him. Without a word, the mighty unicorn blinked down at him. Will placed the whittled eagle back into his pocket and stood. He never felt comfortable with Coraggio, but he never felt comfortable with any of the unicorns, or anyone else for that matter when he came to think about it, except perhaps Rielle. *Did he feel comfortable with himself?* Quickly, he pushed the thought aside.

'I needed time alone,' he muttered defensively, avoiding the unicorn's eyes.

In the distance, a creature howled plaintively. The sound made Will's blood run cold. He shivered, wondering what it meant.

Coraggio threw his head up, his eyes pinpricks, his mane swirling as he poised for flight.

...

When they had first left Wish, in the flash of thought made possible by the First Ones and the Ritual of Return, and found themselves standing at the foothills of the mountain to search for Old's caves, Will had thought it would all be done and over with in a matter of days, but that had not been so.

Too many months had now gone by and they were still searching. Will wondered if they would ever reach the gold in Old's caves, or if the sorcerer would wear them down with his evil surprises and cunning tricks.

If Neves On, Number Seven of the First Ones, or, as he was known in Wish, the Sorcerer of Great Contempt, reached the gold first, then with the added power from the Staff of the Unimaginable in his clutches, the rest of them might be doomed. At least that was what Will had fleetingly overheard the unicorns and the First Ones saying.

...

Coraggio nodded and turned to leave. It was obvious, by the way he did so, that he expected Will to follow. Once more, resentment lashed Will, but he knew he had no choice.

Using the Wand of Time like a humble walking cane for balance, Will clambered over the jumble of jagged rocks and broken stumps that formed the terrain. Fog littered the air like shifting thoughts, making it hard for Will to see Coraggio's white body.

Sunlight coursed through the mist, flushing the valley below in mauve and pink, lighting pockets of snow on the mountainside like meadows of spring flowers.

'It's beautiful isn't it?' Coraggio whispered.

Will nodded and looked away. *Why were they all so nice to him, when he showed them nothing but indifference?*

Walking on, Will stumbled over a jutting log and almost fell, dropping the Wand of Time, which rattled harshly, grating against a rock. Will swore.

Righting himself, he carefully grasped the wand. Before he even thought about it, he rubbed the wood several times in case it had been scratched. Surprising him so much he nearly dropped her again, the wand hummed happily, enchanting the morning with a playful tune. Will stared at the walking wand, not knowing what to do.

Coraggio cleared his throat and waited.

'It... it was an accident,' Will stuttered to the waiting unicorn, as if he owed him an explanation. 'I didn't ask her to sing.'

Coraggio still said nothing. Trusting Will to follow, he stepped into the mist. Will panicked in the murkiness and went to run after him, but once again he stumbled, and once again he dropped the wand. This time, she rolled away from him to tumble eagerly down a slope.

Will looked around for Coraggio but couldn't see him. Pride stopped him from calling for help.

As a hint of the sun's rays climbed the mountain, Will scanned for the missing wand. Golden blobs of sunlight plopped themselves down around him like lazy children after play, finally showing him where the wand had landed. He gaped. She was wedged between two ungainly rocks that jutted crazily over the abyss. If she fell, there was no telling where she would land in the valley far, far below. Again Will looked around for the unicorn, but Coraggio had disappeared. Will opened his mouth to call out but still decided he could not ask for help.

Stepping carefully over a rotting log, he examined the ledge he would need to stand on to reach the wand; it looked flimsy and unstable. As he watched, the Wand of Time shifted a little as a gust of mountain wind puffed at the morning fog. Will panicked. He must not lose Old's gift!

Taking his hat off and laying it neatly on the ground, he quickly arranged himself on his stomach and began crawling toward the edge of the precipice. He inched as far as he thought he could before reaching out with numb, cold fingers. The wand lay just out of reach. Looking down, Will could see to the bottom of the valley as the sun washed the lowlands in peach.

Another gust of wind loosened the wand. Will shifted himself further toward the edge. Triumphantly, his hand met the honey wood. As he grabbed her with clenched, trembling fingers, a stab of sunlight flung sharply into his eyes, briefly blinding him. Unthinking, he raised his other hand to block the glare. His weight pushed down against the ledge. He paused and waited. Nothing happened. With a soft sigh of relief, he began shifting backwards, away from the cliff edge.

Will felt the split, before he heard it. The shift of his weight was just what the rock face needed. With a wrenching snap it cracked and tore with a vigour he could not have expected.

Will and the Wand of Time plunged into the vast, unknown sky. Will called out then but it was too late; there was nothing Coraggio could do for him now. Still clutching the wand as if she and she alone could protect him, he fell toward the valley below.

CHAPTER 3

The watcher calls

Alone and waiting, like two small blobs of mountain rubble, the Imperial Guard Snails, Bibs and little Bobs, shivered within their shells. They were not used to the cold mornings on the mountain, not one bit.

Timidly, little Bobs peeked from his shell, comforted by the sight of Candela. Just then, Bibs stirred. They both gazed adoringly up at the unicorn.

Standing above the snails, Candela breathed warm fragrant air over them, melting the little sticks of ice on their shells. Gusts of her warm breath washed away the fears that little Bobs always awoke with, allowing him to bask in a happy glow. Smiling wordlessly at them, Candela checked that they were both well, then moved as silently as the mist, to wait for Coraggio's return.

A creature howled in the distance. It sounded like a wolf.

Little Bobs shivered. As he always did upon waking and before things became hectic, he thought of his beloved forest, of the ancient trees and their tender silence, the moss he liked to sleep on, the cool waterfalls and gentle streams, and the strips of lazy sunlight that hugged the woodland floor.

...

When the unicorns had decreed that they, the First Ones, and the humans, would need to defend the gold in Old's caves, the group had left Wish together in a rush of thought.

With the walking wands held high and the power from the Ritual of Return, the First Ones and the unicorns had transported them all to the lowlands that led to the slopes of Old's mountain.

Little Bobs and Bibs had no choice in the matter. They had been swept along with the group, whether they'd wanted to be or not. Little Bobs wanted to go back to the forest but there had been no time.

It was unknown at first whether the Sorcerer of Great Contempt even continued to live. After the explosion that had killed Old, the fate of the Staff of the Unimaginable had also remained unknown.

All little Bobs knew was that the unicorns must be the first to find the gold of time.

...

Fully awake, Bibs poked his head out from his shell, yawning hugely.

Peering at his older cousin, Little Bobs noted the signs of sadness that this journey had stamped on Bibs' once cheery face.

Little Bobs took a breath. 'If the unicorns are in such a hurry to find the gold,' he whispered to his older cousin, 'then why do we have to *climb* the mountain? Why don't they just *think* us straight to where we need to go?'

Bibs sighed. Poor little Bobs; he was being forced to grow up fast. He should have been safe and snug in a pocket of forest undergrowth, living a sheltered, happy life, as he deserved.

Bibs examined his young cousin, doing his best to look untroubled.

'I've explained it before,' he began kindly, 'and it's like this.' Bibs cleared his throat. 'Although Rielle has already seen the caves, they say this mountain shifts and changes with many strange moods, and, well, sometimes things are hidden, even from unicorns. I've heard Oobaat and Hope declare that only Old had the courage to live on this mountain.' He paused then continued, pensively.

'I've heard the talk. It seems that Old gave his caves protection and that whatever the Wand of Time does, it cannot be broken. In the orchard that day when... well, when Old gave the wand to Will, he said: *'Things you make they cannot break when you hold the Wand of Time.'*

Bibs glanced at little Bobs to check that he understood.

'Apparently,' he went on, 'the protection is very strong.' Bibs looked around as if he might catch evil lurking and then continued. 'Which in many ways is just as well, otherwise, he... the sorcerer... might already have found the caves and be planning to snatch the gold of time from under our noses.'

Little Bobs nodded. 'So the protection makes it hard to find the caves, even for unicorns and *them*... the First Ones?' He hoped it could all be over soon. He gulped, fought a small tear and snuggled back into his shell, dozing quietly. If he pretended enough, he could imagine he was in another place.

Commotion amongst the unicorns revealed that Coraggio had returned alone.

Without warning, the mountain shook itself as if sensing fleas on its back. It quivered and shuddered as if trying to flick them all off. The group knew what would come next.

The ground beneath them groaned and jumped, as scruffy trees creaked with familiar anguish. Boulders the size of ten trees thundered past, forcing Bibs and little Bobs to flatten their heads, shut their eyes and cling to the ground with tenacity that they didn't know they had when they lived in the safety of the forest. Splinters of broken bushes, trees and clods of earth fell and clumped around the snails as they held their breath and tried not to be afraid.

The unicorns swayed and rocked at the upheaval as if they had been doing it all their lives, but they did so with lowered heads and troubled eyes.

Finally, grunting and shuddering as if happy with its spring cleaning, the mountain settled. For the time being, the unicorns and snails breathed freely again.

As if waiting for the mountain to stop its outburst, the sun flung liquid heat over the group. Quickly, the snails scurried for the cover of shade, although they rejoiced at the end of the cold night.

Bibs and little Bobs were hungry, but food was scarce on the mountain. The unicorns nibbled at tufts of grey and yellow grasses that sprouted mockingly from the

broken red earth but the snails craved the juicy leaves of
the forest. It seemed that only the humans and the First
Ones always had food. Little Bobs knew it was because
of the golden cake tin. Somehow, it never ran out of
something for them to eat.

...

*Before they had all left Wish, Hope and Rielle had
fleetingly returned to the Tower of Dreams for what had been
barely moments. They had returned with the golden cake
tin. Since then, Rielle had carried it hidden under her cloak,
never letting it out of sight. She and the First Ones kept it
vigorously guarded.*

...

Surprisingly, as if created by the snails' own hungry
minds, a large, dewy leaf floated at a leisurely pace
straight past Bibs and little Bobs. Little Bobs' eyes lit
up like candles in the night. The leaf must have been
dislodged from some bush above them when the
mountain had rocked and rolled.

The snails snuck quick peeks at each other, and then
eyed the green leaf as it dipped and turned and rose
above their heads. Saliva dripped unappealingly from
them. In a mad dash, both snails bolted after it, chasing
randomly, their eyes on the prize!

Almost reaching it, little Bobs leapt into the air, his
antennae pointed keenly and his mouth poised to bite.
Eagerly, he realised the leaf was much bigger than he had
at first supposed and hungrily, he leaped a little higher

than he had intended. He bit and held the leaf, as success filled his heart.

At that moment the mountain coughed, grunted and spat, sending a gust of unwelcome wind to flurry amongst its visitors. And so it was that instead of landing neatly back down, little Bobs and the giant leaf were carried on the wind, out of sight. Just as he realised what was happening, little Bobs heard a whisper.

Rielle… called an unknown voice.

CHAPTER 4

I am Neves On - Number Seven of the First Ones
But they call me the Sorcerer of Great Contempt

Neves On, Number Seven of the First Ones, squinted with livid eyes at the cave he called home. The first gentle whispers of dawn were emerging, but he hated the sun and his lip curled in scorn. He paced, as was his usual way, proven by the long groove etched into the stone of the floor. A bunk lay untouched at the centre of the cave. Neves On never slept; at best, he dozed.

Thoughts consumed and churned through his mind with poison fed by aeons of time. *His purpose was being wasted!* He had prepared his power, but for what reason? He was trapped in a place that was of no use to him, a place where he was unwillingly confined. He ground his teeth so hard that the sound filled the chamber.

For the hundredth time his gaze fell upon the Staff of the Unimaginable. She lay still, in her white fashion, unable to shine a light from her wood. Dark unnatural grooves marked her where she had been thrown from the explosion that had rocked her core, the same explosion that had killed Old, Number Twenty Three of the First Ones, Eerht Ytnewt On.

Neves On felt little triumph. He would have preferred the eruption to have killed Hope or Oobaat, or best of all, a unicorn, but that fool Number Twenty Three had chosen to be a hero!

He studied the white wand, contemplating the scores that marked her. He went to pick her up but thought better of it. The darkened scars were his doing. He had created the devastation that had ignited her until she coruscated in an explosion that even he could not have imagined.

His brothers had provoked him - it was their fault - and now he wondered if she would ever be as powerful as she once was. He reached out as if to take her in his hand, but instead, he turned and stormed furiously from the cave.

A deep wound on his leg was open and sore. He too had paid a price from the battle in the almond orchard. It was excruciating when he walked, but gritting his teeth, he strode on. He glanced down at his right hand. A mark stretched across its breadth. His brothers, Enin On and Eno On, Hope and Oobaat, had surprised him with their crafty tactics of warfare.

He frowned, clenching the painful fist, despite the agony it caused him. He could heal himself with power should he want to, but it was better to feel the pain for a while longer, so he could remain vengeful and filled with spite.

Nothing was as he wanted it to be!

He stormed with sharp steps through the landscape of Wish, bearing a scowl so menacing that young birds scattered at the look in his eye, and trees held themselves ready for his unpredictable assaults. Some days, he practised evil magic and tore whole forests from their roots, as if it were his right.

Life recoiled from the Sorcerer of Great Contempt. He respected nothing, it was well understood. History had shown this time and again.

His steps took him to the usual place that drew him irresistibly each day as he seethed with futile resentment. He stopped and looked up. Soaring with intention and powerful dignity, the Tower of Dreams stood on hallowed ground.

Facing each other like gladiators in a long, time-scored battle, Neves On and the tower understood each other's purpose.

With something like a sigh, the fortress settled to wait. The Sorcerer of Great Contempt could not enter its doors but the tower knew he would not give up trying. Whispers penetrated the Tower's deepest nexus. Messages ran with utmost speed and urgency through the hidden, silent corners of its corridors, leaving no hall or room in doubt as to the enemy outside.

A blast of energy radiated from the tower, and for one searing, swift moment, Neves On was blinded. He cried out, as he always did, yet he knew the tower would show him mercy even as he hated it for doing so. Whispers reached out to him, whispers from the tower's eternal keepers.

'Go away, lost one,' they sighed, 'go away. You can never enter here. You can never enter here.'

Gasping, the sorcerer covered his ears. For moments longer he skulked by the moat, trying to peer into Hope's room, but boiling moat mud sat on the window sills, and the force of the potion thrust him backward with a heave. He shook his fist at the fortress, baring his lips in a fierce grin.

'One day,' he vowed, 'I will enter your doors!'

The whispers laughed, not unkindly. 'Never,' they sighed, 'never! You cannot enter here, for this is the place of truth.'

As if to confirm the whispers, the little moat beat hostile waters to send him on his way. The tower's whispers ceased.

Neves On assessed the moat. He had almost stood on its bridge once. He knew that if he thought about it long enough, he would find what he wanted. He turned. It would have to wait. In a rage of spiteful conflict, he flung poison to taint the soil around him, leaving small patches of corruption like a trail of disease, where he walked.

Once again in his dim cave, Neves On paced, seething. Glaring at the Staff of the Unimaginable, he tapped her smooth white wood with a tremor in his hand that surprised and challenged him. She lay still. As always, she would not sing at his touch. Five deep cuts bruised her beauty and Neves On wondered if they would go away with time. With more than a tremor, he picked her up.

Would she still have power? Would he still be able to command her after what he had done?

With an almost gentle hand, he touched one of the deep cuts in her wood that looked like a dark sore against her whiteness. He gasped, flinched, and drew back, almost dropping her. Where he touched the blackened scar, she burned him with a painful scorch!

'Well, my little toy,' he sneered, trying to hide his

hostile surprise, 'well, at least you're alive.'

The wand lay silent. Discomforted, Neves On briefly panicked. Her ruinous scars disturbed him. How much had she changed? He peered at her with thoughtful eyes. Without her, his plans could go astray.

...

The heart of the Staff of the Unimaginable belonged to unicorns; she was their white wand, but the memory was distant and she barely remembered it to be so.

Pain seared through her wounds and tormented her with disbelief. She had been made with love and trust and gentle caring but there was nothing left of that in her world now... there hadn't been for a long time.

She knew she carried power though, and before the explosion, also great beauty. Before the battle in the almond orchard, nothing had scarred her pure white wood and no mark had scorned her ancient truth.

Buried within the staff was so much knowledge that it would take thousands of years to unravel. She was made by unicorns at the beginning of time, from a part of the Tree of Life, as was the Book of Divination, well before The Circle of Light had formed the eleven minor wands that were given to the First Ones, much later on.

The Staff of the Unimaginable was formed where knowledge and pure love met, by the mother of all unicorns, Candela.

In her deepest truth, the Staff of the Unimaginable was not sure how she had been stolen by the Sorcerer of Great Contempt. One moment she was safe, watched by the herd and Oobaat, Number One of the First Ones, and then, in a strange twist that must only have come about by cunning, she was in the clutches of Neves On.

At first she thought if she did not sing, then he would send her back, but he kept her nonetheless, somehow discovering the secret that made it possible to use her power. Even the unicorn wand could not refuse the command of whoever held her. Wands were made to serve, not to rule, and therein lay their defenceless secret.

The Staff of the Unimaginable felt the five wounds upon her wood pierce through to her deepest centre. Time went into making of the wands: time to lock into the surface the layers of knowledge that seeped to their core. The wounding soiled her.

Where the cruel explosion had altered her, it robbed knowledge and information from her knowing. She was no longer who she had been. She was changed forever.

...

'Live,' Neves On whispered, 'we have work to do, my pretty one. Live! I need you. Do not let me down!'

Fury boiled within him. He stifled it. Perhaps there was another way.

Give me your life
Give me your power
Don't hold back
Get back on track

White wood wand
You are mine to command
Be reborn
There is work this morn

I am number seven, Neves On
Unravel your secrets
I command you to obey
Come what may

Neves On waited. Squinting with a mercenary look of anticipation, he held his breath and waited. Minutes went by and he became agitated. He tried again.

White wand
Held by my hand
Serve me well
You know you can

Leave the past
Far behind
Give me your power
To last for all time!

The wand pulsed a red glow from her centre. Neves On hissed in victory. She was still his to rule! She was still the most powerful wand, and all things were possible again. He strode with her to the doorway of his cave. Looking triumphantly outward, he sent a thought to the tower.

I will break you. I will break your secrets and claim them.

The Tower of Dreams caught the thought. It rustled briefly. Neves On, it knew, suffered from delusion.

CHAPTER 5

For he who falls

Will partly awoke from what felt like a deep sleep. He was cold but not shivering. In his left hand he clenched the Wand of Time so tightly that his fingers were rigid and cramped. He took a deep breath and continued to rest, his eyes closed. Something tickled his arm. Drowsily, he brushed at it, but it didn't go away. He grunted, irritated, and then fell back into a doze.

He awoke fully some time later and made a listless face. Any minute now the unicorns would call him for the reluctant climb up the mountain. Something tickled his arm again. Annoyed, he opened his eyes and looked up. An eagle was perched beside him, its sharp hunter's eyes staring straight into his.

'Argh!' Will choked.

With a swift movement, Will swivelled to his feet, barely managing to steady himself. He looked down, swayed, and cried out. He began to shiver. His knees shook and his hands trembled, and the fear in his belly burned. He shut his eyes and then opened them. This was not a dream. Leaning back onto the slip of mountain behind his back, sick terror clawed his throat.

He remembered. He had fallen! He had saved the Wand of Time, but in so doing, he had fallen. That was the last thing he could recall.

The platform he stood on was only a matter of a few paces all round, a mere out-thrust of rock that jutted like a hand from the mountain's side. It provided no shelter, not even a stunted tree or shrub. Will took a quick, sickening peek at the valley below. It was so far away that only a blur of colour showed, offering no shapes of particular meaning, as the sun splashed shadows on the distant valley floor.

Will shot a glance at the eagle. 'Go away,' he pleaded, 'shoo!'

The eagle stayed. It continued to pin him with warm auburn eyes then blinked, looked around and turned to fully face him before inching closer.

Will recoiled. 'Get away from me!' he screamed. 'Get away!' Something like a sob rocked his words, which floated desolately to meet endless sky.

The eagle moved closer.

Will was not short, but the eagle's head was as high as his waist. Will squeezed himself as far as he could to the end of the ledge, until he could go no further. The eagle took quick short steps until it stood right beside him. It looked up at him as if daring him to move. Will wondered if the ledge would crumble and send him plummeting to his end.

'What do you want?' he wheezed to the bird.

The eagle settled itself then. Becoming comfortable, it nestled down.

Will's mind spun. Sharp tugs of wind blustered around him, and he had to focus not to fall. He shut his eyes and leaned back onto the mountain.

Somehow he had landed on this ledge and had remained unharmed.

Sweat poured from his brow but he dared not move a muscle to wipe it away. He began to shiver in earnest. Chilled by the wind and sweating from fear, he clutched the Wand of Time as if she, and she alone, could save him.

Exhausted with anxiety and cold, his body stiff and sore, Will caught himself dozing just before he began to fall. With a gasp, he clenched the mountain wall behind him, digging his fingernails into the rock so deeply that he almost dropped the wand. His legs shook uncontrollably.

The eagle did not move.

Desperately, Will also wanted to crouch, like the bird. He needed to rest his aching limbs but the dozing eagle took up most of the ledge. Will shut his eyes in shock, and focused on his breathing.

The day was blurred and miserable, passing slowly. Time seemed to jolt as the air grew cooler and night drew near. Finally, Will opened his eyes. The eagle was gone! As soundless as it was daunting, it had left the ledge and he hadn't even known.

How long had it been gone? With a sigh that caught in his throat, Will collapsed and drew his knees up to his chest. Silently, like the eagle, the sun withdrew and plunged Will into darkness. Oddly, the dark was less terrifying.

With the first fear gone, Will began to feel hungry. Soon the thought uppermost in his mind was the need to eat and drink, but even as the thought began to control him, he realised it didn't matter anyhow; he was bound to soon be dead. Anger clutched at his stomach and resentment scratched him. If they had never come to the mountain then none of this would have happened!

There was no way off the ledge. Will thought back to the reason he had fallen. For a blinding moment, he hated the wand with a loathsome vengeance. Groping in the dark, he kneeled, and prepared to hurl her away from him. He wanted to hurt her, to be rid of her, to let her fall to the valley below and have nothing more to do with her. He drew back to fling her, but the Wand of Time did a wonderful thing. She began to sing.

For he who falls and also fails
Yet rises, despite hardship and travail
Does hail from kings and kingdoms far away
Let no hindrance stop his passage
Nor lay him low or halt his destiny
By either night or day

Into the blackness and beyond, she continued her song.

A time must come
For truth to call
A mirror, a lesson, or a fall
Disbelief of the truth of time

Brings swift misfortune
And years of pain and contemplation

Believe Will, Willful James
Believe or reap your sadness and pain
Let the wise ones of the world
Teach you, train you, heal your wounds
Reject the truth and prepare to pay
For the error of your way!

Her melting tones swept into the night and settled gently to end on a sweet high note. White light pulsed softly at her core, warming Will with a spark of hope.

Gasping, Will collapsed backwards and sat down again. He thought of Old, as if the First One were there with him on the ledge. In a quick, grappling movement, there was something Will had to find out. Tenderly, he pulled a small wooden carving of an eagle from his pocket, the one that Old had whittled for him by the fireside when he had offered Will tea for sadness. Elation moved Will; he hadn't lost it in the fall!

He wanted to tell Old, in that moment, that the wand had sung for him and that she had served him and saved him from a terrible moment of aching despair. For some reason he didn't understand, he also thought of Rielle as she had looked, leaning over Old when he lay dying. Her eyes had mirrored in those moments, how Will was feeling now. For the first time in his life, Will understood, really understood, how someone else felt.

He drew his knees up and rested his head on them as loneliness of unbearable intensity flowed through him. He wondered if he would starve first or go slowly mad. Desperate, he tapped the wand as he had seen Old do.

'Sing,' he whispered fiercely, 'sing to me.'

Without a moment's hesitation the Wand of Time chanted with joy.

Although we as men
Draw breath and build castles in the air
And spend our time fleeing death
Life awaits us in the wings

Although we as unicorn
Do vow and honour to protect
And spend our time sowing deeds
Life belongs to those we help and to those in need

Although we as First Ones
Watch the gates of being
And spend our time in art of weaving
Life begins in our timely actions and in our knowledge from
the beginning

And so having said
In the end
The challenge lies for all of us
Not in big, but in little things.

She stopped, and her white light flamed a solution

to the night's dark side. Will wondered what it meant. She sang of humans and unicorns and First Ones and challenges.

'Not in big, but in little things,' Will whispered out loud. The chant raged inside his mind. What did she mean by it all?

Just then, as silently as it had gone, the eagle landed on the ledge, and sat beside him like a long, lost friend.

CHAPTER 6

When darkness flows to blight what's right

Rana the frog had changed. Watching over the wishing pond was not what he had expected. There was no glory. He had imagined it would be a much more glamorous job, but belatedly, he was discovering it was not glamorous at all. He watched and waited as creatures came and went, performing his duties of gatekeeper as meticulously as he could and with the best intentions. But Rana was lonely for his mentor.

Oobaat had been gone a very long time. Rana wondered when Oobaat would return and hoped it would be soon. Odd things had started happening, and in his limited wisdom, Rana did not understand their meaning.

Rana looked up. A great grey owl was sitting in an ancient lichen-brushed tree near the wishing pond. That had become its habit for some time now, almost every moment of the night and day. At the other end of the pond sat an ancient Imperial Guard Snail, the one who was known as Bobs.

Neither snail nor owl ever spoke to Rana and they hardly made a sound. They watched and waited, as if they knew something that he did not.

Each day Rana wanted to say hello to them, but their patient, silent vigil seemed to ban him from their thoughts.

The grey she owl would bring her mate morsels to eat, and then, as if in pity, she would carry grasses in her claws and drop them at the snail's feet.

For swift seconds only, the great grey owl would swoop to the pond to drink, and then regain his perch to watch and listen pensively.

Days turned to night and nights turned to day and still there was no word from Oobaat. Finally Rana decided that perhaps Oobaat would not return at all, perhaps it would remain with him, Rana the frog, to be gatekeeper to the wishing pond, forever. The thought made him sad. The very thing he had hoped and longed for was, in reality, a lonesome chore.

And so time passed in the forest. Glimmering softly, it shimmered in its hidden world of green and gold, safe and protected and wrapped in its natural layer of the Ritual of Return.

One morning, as Rana pretended not to watch them, the great grey owl swooped to join the wizened snail. Rana peeked at them curiously. This was new behaviour.

Almost immediately, a flock of thousands of white squawking birds flew low with furious intent across the pond and through the forest. Their wings pounded the air with such urgency, that they sounded like a galloping herd.

Rana goggled. *What did these things mean?*

A swift breeze rattled the trees of the forest, and leaves rustled with unusual vigour as branches groaned.

Rana frowned. The forest was never restless. It grew and changed with a quiet, gentle passion that filled the very air and soil with nourishment and joy. It never rustled and it certainly never groaned! Troubled, he looked over at the owl and the snail.

They were deep in conversation that even Rana, with his knack for eavesdropping, could not hear. It was then that they turned toward him and watched him steadily, as if by doing so they might learn something they needed to know.

Uneasily, Rana tried to carry on but each time he looked to the corner of the pond, the owl and snail stared wordlessly at him. Finally, he couldn't take it anymore. Gathering his courage, he defiantly hopped directly in front of them and stopped. No one spoke.

Eventually, the owl cleared his throat.

'My name is Hoot,' he began in a deep, low voice that hinted that his message was of a subtle menace. 'I expect you might know me from the time gone by when my friend here, and I, travelled with Benny and Bibs, to Wish.'

Rana blinked. *Of course! The very first time that Benny the unicorn had gone to Wish, he had been accompanied by two Imperial Guard snails and a great grey owl.* He nodded.

'I see,' Hoot went on, 'that you are not so quick with your answers these days.' In the pause that followed, Rana wondered whether he had been complimented or not.

'Good,' the owl went on, 'good. It seems that being in charge of the pond has taught you something after all.' He held up a wing at the look of annoyance on Rana's face. 'No, no, it wasn't meant to offend,' he sighed, 'merely to let you know why we've been watching you for so long.'

Rana swallowed and his large red eyes bulged. 'You've been watching *me?*' he gulped. 'I thought you were doing something much more mysterious.'

Hoot raised an eyebrow and tilted his head. 'You are mysterious, my friend,' he drawled. 'Trust me when I tell you so.'

Rana drew a breath to answer, but Bobs interrupted with a burst of annoyance.

'Oh for goodness sake,' Bobs barked, 'the Ritual of Return is under threat!'

Rana gaped, in disbelief. 'Impossible,' he stammered, 'that would be impossible.' He stared from Hoot to Bobs and shook his head. 'Is that possible?'

'I'm afraid so,' Hoot responded matter-of-factly, 'I'm afraid so.' He repeated the words, almost as if he needed to convince himself.

'But, what can do such a thing?' Rana roared.

Owl and snail exchanged an unhappy glance.

Hoot shuddered. 'It's not a what, but a who. We met him once, and whispers are reaching our ears to tell us he is now stronger than we thought, and somehow different. Something unfamiliar has happened that we don't understand.'

'But, but, nothing can harm the forest,' Rana gasped. 'Surely nothing bad can come here? This is unicorn territory after all; it's sacred and held in trust.' He paused fearfully, looking timidly over his shoulder.

Hoot and Bobs said nothing.

Rana glared sharply at them. 'Whispers? Did you

mention whispers? I haven't heard any whispers! At least I don't think I have.'

Hoot nodded. 'Ah, yes,' he replied uncertainly, 'yes the forest is sacred and should be untouched by harm, and safe, certainly, as it is cushioned by the Ritual of Return, *but....* '

Rana hopped closer to the two. 'But what?' he urged as the snail and owl pondered. 'But what?' Rana bellowed, forgetting he was gatekeeper now, and should behave accordingly.

'Don't shout,' snapped Bobs. 'We heard you! I may be old but I'm not deaf, you know!' He frowned, his brow becoming a wrinkled mass of crossness. Pushing his nose into Rana's face he stared unflinchingly at him.

Rana stepped back. 'But what?' he whispered. 'What aren't you telling me? This is unicorn territory. Nothing can harm the forest!'

'Sssh,' Hoot insisted, 'shoosh, stop your confounded hounding and let me explain what I know!' He flashed Rana an impatient look and in that moment the forest rustled with greater agitation.

Rana, Hoot and Bobs peered upward, as boughs groaned loudly. A resounding crack snapped through the air. The three of them jumped.

In a moment of sudden hope, Rana turned to the others. 'It might be Oobaat returning!' he cried.

Hoot silenced him with a preoccupied look.

'Oobaat has never made an unnecessary sound in all his life,' Bobs grumbled through clenched lips. 'Quickly, let's move over there!'

Without another word they scuttled to take shelter.

The forest whispered, and a flutter of life erupted as all manner of creatures scurried to hide. Another loud snap split the silence and then the forest was still. A long time went by. Nothing moved. But this time the lack of movement felt forced.

Just as Rana began to relax, the pond bubbled and bounced. A loud call split the air, and laughter, devious and joyless, echoed, bouncing off trees and rocks. The white light of the Ritual of Return dimmed and trembled. The undergrowth moaned and quivered.

Rana, Hoot and Bobs held their breath.

An enormous ancient tree began to rock and sway, its trunk bending and bowing as if it might snap in two.

Rana held back a sob. Who would torment an ancient keeper this way? Who would wrack the forest and put fear in its path? Hearts pounding, they all waited.

Any moment now, the tree could snap like a sapling and be destroyed!

Fearlessly, the tree fought its attacker. Valiantly, it twisted and turned, boldly fighting its invisible assailant with massive, white, time-worn limbs.

Rana couldn't bear to watch. The tree was being pulled to breaking point.

Surely, at any moment it would snap and fatally fall, laying everything in its path to waste?

'Now!' cried Hoot bravely, surprising Rana with his call. 'Now! Now! Now!'

Then, in a moment that none of them would ever forget, every being in the forest rushed fearlessly from places of safety and hiding, with teeth bared and talons ready, beaks and wings and bodies bared. Not knowing what they were fighting didn't stop the creatures of the forest. Swarming and rallying around the ancient tree, they pounced and pummelled its invisible assailant with all their might, risking their defenceless, brave lives.

A loud screech filled the air. It chilled Rana's blood, even as he also roared and croaked and jumped around. Again the screech rent the air, and then the tree stood motionless.

Hush filled the forest.

Tall and stately, the tree rested quietly. The Ritual of Return was intact! The undergrowth settled and the pond became tranquil. Whatever had just happened, the forest would not be plundered. The small creatures cheered. The forest was still sacred!

'We're safe,' Hoot called. 'Whatever it was, it's gone for now.'

Everyone gazed at the ancient tree with breathless relief, hearts still pumping.

'How do you know?' Rana gulped, still uneasy.

'Because,' Bobs countered, 'nothing can wrestle with the Tree of Life for long, and win!' He gazed lovingly at the unbeaten monarch and then went on in a softer tone. 'That tree was here before unicorns… even before Candela, the mother of all unicorns, was herself a thought.'

They looked up in awe. The tree stood tall and silent now, somewhat daunting, yet quietly humble. The Ritual of Return poured steadily from its branches.

CHAPTER 7

Forever changed

Neves On clutched the Staff of the Unimaginable as she flared a red glow from her centre. He laughed aloud. He was back on track! With a word, he healed his damaged leg, but allowed the welt to remain across his hand. It would remind him not to underestimate his brothers again. Taking one last look at the cave he hated to call home, he sneered at its humble comforts and strode out from the entrance, vowing never to return.

This was his moment. For many hundreds of years, he had waited for this.

Neves On wanted to live forever; was there something wrong with that? What were the mere few thousand years the First Ones normally had as their lot, when he could gain life eternal and become powerful beyond belief?

Grinning broadly from a demeanour so frightening that it made leaves wilt and sent small animals to hide, there was one last thing he wanted to do in Wish. *Would he have time?* He strode toward the Tower of Dreams.

As he gazed at something only he could see, Neves On's footsteps slowed then abruptly, he stopped.

Excitement flared within him. Cradling the Staff of the Unimaginable as if she were an offering, and holding her carefully so that her burnt and charred scars could not scorch him, he focused on his foremost task.

In a voice that lilted in an eerie sing-song, he began to chant.

Send me hence
Send me far
Let me wander
Hold no bars

I rule the wind
In outward places
I govern wolves
And with them change faces

Let me free
Let me be
Let me maim
And run from here

I call wolf
Of mottle coat
To be my teeth
For a unicorn throat

Be thorough, be quick
Make no mistake
Add vile poison
Defile and take!

Neves On uttered the chant not once, but several times.

The Staff of the Unimaginable glowed at her centre. *She was using her power.* He had unlocked the secret to her again, but this time, she was helping him to destroy a unicorn! Did she know, he wondered, what it was he had asked? Did she understand? Did she realise that it was a command to destroy her makers? Neves On caught his breath and grinned from darkened lips. If she could be commanded to help kill one unicorn, then perhaps his power was endless. Perhaps he could destroy the entire herd. Precious success surged through his sinister, dismal heart.

Gripping her white wood in an iron fist, he felt her power flush through him. In that moment of soaring triumph, he was unprepared for the wand's next move. For the first time ever while Neves On held her, she spoke.

It was more a sound than words, streaming from her in a metallic shriek, and the five scores which deeply cut and wounded her pure wood glowed bitter red to match her centre.

Even as she responded to Neves On's chant, she twisted in his grasp and brought one of her charred scores to rest on his hand. It burned him as surely as if the wolf he was using in the outside world to wreak havoc had attacked *him!*

With a shriek to match the wand, the Sorcerer of Great Contempt stared at his hand in disbelief. It was raw and open and showed the marks of teeth. His mind raced. How could that be? He gaped and dropped the wand even as he staggered with the intensity of her burn.

Once again she uttered a sound. It was quieter this

time, but still, no melody or words flowed from her. She lay quietly then, with the five dark scores simply black and charred and no longer red.

Neves On had never experienced such pain. He feared that the intensity of it would drive him mad.

'Heal,' he screeched, but the mutilation did not change. 'Heal!' he bellowed as real fear clutched him. 'Heal! Heal! Heal!' His hand remained tattered and torn. With livid eyes, he stared vacantly at the wand.

'You,' he gasped, 'you gave me your power but then you maimed me!'

With an effort he could not believe possible, he remained standing on his feet, dizzy and weak, his dark lips moving, yet speechless. The inexplicable truth dawned on him.

She was changed! She was changed from the scores that defaced her. She was altered through to her core.

He sunk to his knees, never taking his eyes from her. He needed her. He needed her allegiance more than ever!

His chant should have torn the Ritual of Return. Old's gold and eternal life might soon be his. Perplexed, and unaccustomed to the feeling, he gawped at the Staff of the Unimaginable.

Still weak, he whispered another spell to make his new wound heal. This time he was lucky: the flesh of his hand closed over, although a remnant of pain still ached within.

Desperate with a need to hurry, yet surprised by the flicker of terror she provoked within him, the sorcerer reached with wary fingers to pick the wand up from where she lay. Briefly, she glowed red again as her scores flared, then quickly went dark. Neves On handled her with care.

The scores were his fault - he had made them happen - but she was doing something no wand was meant to do. What was this uncanny defiance? *Could she be thinking for herself?* He shook his head. Impossible!

'Speak,' he whispered, 'speak to me! Tell me what I need to know.'

The white wand did not speak, but like a warning, she went warm to his touch. The sorcerer prepared to fling her down, but she lay dormant in his hand.

'I need you now,' he rasped. 'I need you more than ever. I am your master. It is me who commands *you*, do you hear? It is *me* who commands.' He watched her move slightly. It felt like a caution.

Neves On stood to his full height. Desperately, he wanted to lash out, to hurl her. He wanted to break her slender white wood, destroy her, explode her with a bolt of power. Yet softly, as if she were the tender love of his cold heart, he held her with firm, gentle fingers as far from her wounds as he could grasp.

Confounded, he proceeded toward the Tower of Dreams.

The Staff of the Unimaginable hummed in a soft voice that no one heard. Fleetingly she glowed at her centre, and the glow was as white as the white of her wood.

Neves On brooded with a rage of such immense proportion at the unfortunate turn of events that his thoughts sent dark green corruption into the air, leeched from each and every one of his pores. The darkness tainted the atmosphere of Wish, forming a gathering of blemished clouds that began to discolour the sun.

He hated his brothers and he would make them pay! Sometimes, he thought he hated them more than he could ever hate the unicorn herd. In their righteousness, his brothers had stood by and done nothing to stop the unicorns from exiling him to Wish. It was their fault. His brothers should have fought for him to remain free. They had betrayed him.

Maddened with anger, Neves On hissed abhorrence to the ones who had wronged him.

Break
Break
Crush and bruise!

Maim
Maim
Injure and ruin!

Slam
Slam
Destroy and wound!

All that belongs to my brothers
I will steal
I will take!

Let me plunder
Give me success,
So be it, let their hearts break!

He repeated the litany over and over as he strode, determined and unyielding, until he reached the tower. Darkness was infusing Wish so fully from his thoughts that even he could barely see.

Squinting sourly through the billowing miasma of dark corrosive sky, the sorcerer noticed a rainbow dragon standing by Hope's windows. In the darkness, the dragon could not see him. Greater rage choked Neves On. He despised Rainbow Dragons! Viciously he muttered:

Interfering lizard with wings
Be crushed
Be broken
Be of no use
Crawl on your belly with grovelling things!

Bored, the Sorcerer of Great Contempt promptly forgot the dragon and turned to gaze at the tower's turrets. He tried to break the barriers of Hope's room with a searing thought, stretching his cunning and the white wand's authority, all the while sensing the tower's discomfort and rejection.

But what was this? Neves On paused. *The tower would have to wait. His mind was tugged toward a greater prize. Immediate, pressing business called! It was time!*

In a jolt of new, vital information, he promptly forgot Hope's room. He cast one last look toward the Tower of Dreams and sniggered. He sensed the shuddering of those inside.

'I know you are there,' he whispered chillingly, as he

turned away, 'and I will come back for you.'

Then, blotting all else from his mind, Neves On, Number Seven of the First Ones, prepared himself for his greatest victory.

The wolf pack ran with their own business to attend to as they had for thousands of years, in perfect harmony, on the mountain they loved to live on.

One wolf, however, stopped. Leaving the pack, the mottle-coated wolf turned away. It was time to do its master's bidding.

♦♦♦

CHAPTER 8

Be careful where you tread
On a misty winter's night

Feeling strong enough to stand after her brush with death, Rielle was forced to sit again by the furore of the mountain's latest outburst. Huddling with the First Ones, Pud and Benny, she did what she always did when the mountain threw a tantrum: she thought of Old.

After all, if Old had lived on and inside the mountain for thousands of years, surely their group could survive, despite the mountain's ferocious sense of humour. It was grumpy, that was all, and big. It was a huge, grumpy, itchy, scratching lump of dirt that moaned and groaned and did not like to be intruded.

What frightened Rielle, much more than the mountain at its worst, was wondering what the Sorcerer of Great Contempt might do next.

Above them, a massive tree crashed, thundering past too closely for comfort, throwing Rielle and Pud against Benny, who swayed easily with the strain. At last, the mountain gave one last grunt, belched un-fetchingly, and left them to recover.

Red and black dust smothered them all from head to

foot, and as they shook and brushed themselves, Rielle wondered if she would ever be clean again. She knew she would have to find water so that she could wash her blood-stained tunic, or risk attracting all sorts of evil creatures.

A brief memory of the stalking wolf flashed through her mind. Chilled, she squeezed Pud fiercely. Her dog almost never left her side; he was her dearest friend. It wasn't the first time he had saved her life! Pud grinned back at her as if he didn't know the meaning of a growl. His huge tan eyebrows wiggled and he nudged his mistress in a fit of sneezing and joy.

The sun soared through the morning.

Rielle…

Rielle gasped. No matter how often she heard it, she was still not used to the voice that came out of nowhere, to whisper her name. She looked up at the First Ones and Benny. With a nod of their heads, they confirmed that they, too, had heard it.

Hope called the voice her *watcher*. It was a fitting description: it called her name before something unusual, or immense, occurred.

Benny stood tall, his ears pricked for the slightest sound, as Pud sniffed the air with his hackles raised. Oobaat and Hope stood poised, their walking wands up, their eyes and ears on full alert.

Out of the blue, a rock fell from above to land at Rielle's feet. The rock sneezed and groaned and appeared to be wrapped in a large leaf. The eyes of the group fell curiously on it. The rock bumped about a bit and then grew a face.

'Little Bobs!' Rielle cried. 'What are you doing here? I thought you were safe with the unicorn herd.'

Little Bobs peered shamefacedly at the enquiring eyes surrounding him.

'I flew and then I fell,' he whispered, blushing bright red. He wasn't going to tell them that he'd been greedy and then caught a ride with a leaf!

'What do you mean, you flew?' Rielle asked, but little Bobs hid inside his shell and she knew there would be no more talk from him for a while.

Rielle…

Hope grimaced cautiously. 'Your watcher calls, Rielle,' he breathed urgently, 'be …. '

Hope never finished what he began to say, for at that very moment, the mottle-coated wolf reappeared, charging with fantastic speed from behind some newly flung boulders. With teeth grotesquely bared, the wolf leapt wildly at Benny and in one swift movement, its salivating fangs found their mark and bit deeply into the soft flesh of Benny's neck. As quickly as it had come, the wolf bolted from sight, leaving the group gaping in shocked disbelief.

Incredulous at the boldness of the strike, everyone stood momentarily dazed as Benny buckled and fell to his knees, his breath rasping and raw. In less than a moment his eyes closed, and he lay still.

Oobaat and Hope banged the Staff of Life and the Wand of Faith onto the ground and called out in a shout of power.

Horror dismayed Rielle, as she tried to believe what was happening. Helplessly she called out, even as she watched him fall to the ground.

'Benny! Benny! Benny!'

During what felt like hours of desolation and loss, and

yet was less than a skip of a second, the unicorn herd appeared in all their numbers to surround them on the placid, sun-drenched slope.

'Cursed poison in its filthy fangs!' Coraggio exclaimed with one look at the scene.

Without another word, the herd gathered around Benny and focused on the Ritual of Return. Hope and Oobaat coursed blue light from their wands into the little unicorn. If they all worked quickly enough, perhaps the damage could be undone!

Little Bobs sniffled. They had been distracted because of him. He had chased and clung to the giant leaf because of his silly greed and if they hadn't been watching him, they might have sensed the wolf's daring attack and done something to stop it from happening.

Pud paced, hackles raised and teeth bared, as if willing the creature to return.

Wading through the herd and flinging herself down, Rielle reached out to touch Benny. *His breathing had stopped!* She could not take her hand away. This was Benny before her; Benny who had shown her the way to herself; Benny, who had given her the truth of unicorns. She shuddered. First Old, and now this! *Surely, this could never happen to Benny? Not to a unicorn!*

In the moments of dread that followed, Rielle remembered that unicorns were immortal, but only inside the confines of their beloved forest. Here, in the outside world, they were flesh and blood like everyone else.

The Staff of Life and the Wand of Faith began to hum and then unasked, they began to sing, their voices cloaked in tears.

Be careful where you tread
On a misty winter's night
For stories tell of things we dread
But they may not be right

Be careful where you tip-toe
On a morning kissed with spring
For you may see the unicorn
As she stops to breathe dew in

Be careful where you stand and sing
Should you do so near a mountain stream
For you may lose your heart my friend
To the mysteries of a dream

Be careful where you stand
If your back is turned to moon
For you may feel the fleeting breath
Of a passing unicorn

Be careful what you think
And when you say you ought
For unicorns they know your heart
And see into your thoughts

Be careful, be careful
Do not rush or force
For otherwise you will never know
How a unicorn kiss is bought.

In the dark silence of the aftermath, nothing moved.

Like statues, the group perched on the friendless mountainside, and for lonely, unblessed seconds, they became ornaments of the mountain's making. An eagle circled above. With pealing, silken tones it seemed to ask a question. Valuable moments jumped and skipped in jagged flashes to all who stood and kneeled by Benny the little unicorn in his moment of dire need, as blue and white light danced with shivering force to suck the curse from him.

Rielle did not move. She kneeled with her hands on his neck and shed no tears; grief was taking too large a hand inside of her for that. She simply sat and looked at Benny's dear beloved face and added what she could to the moment, with a quiet prayer of her own.

Pud had not moved from his defensive stance. He stood looking outside the circle, waiting, in case the wolf returned, as little Bobs remained wide-eyed, apart and alone.

There was no need for Pud to wait and watch, however, for the damage was complete. The wolf had obeyed his master and was long gone.

…

In the vital, epic moments that followed, Neves On, the Sorcerer of Great Contempt, clutched the Staff of the Unimaginable. Triumphantly, with a vision that showed him the outside world, he saw what had been done. He grinned.

The Ritual of Return was broken!

♦♦♦

CHAPTER 9

I wait and watch the world go by

Sunlight filtered in delicate tendrils through the windows of Hope's room. Far, the butterfly, sighed noisily. A long time had gone by and she often grew lonely. Worry flitted across her tender features for her beloved mentor, Hope, *Enin On*, Number Nine of the First Ones.

The Tower of Dreams was not the same without Hope. Nothing was the same anymore. She wished that she was with him and the others. The last time she had seen him was after the battle of the almond orchard when Hope and Rielle had briefly returned to the tower, bringing Far back with them.

...

'You will stay behind, butterfly,' Hope had announced as he placed her on his window sill. 'Someone must guard the sixteenth door, and that someone will be you.'

Far had argued briefly. Why her? What about helping to find Rielle's dream? What about... all sorts of things? But Hope's mind would not be changed.

Picking up Old's golden cake tin and handing it to Rielle, he had given Far a fond parting look.

He had turned to Rielle then. 'It's gold, Rielle, so we must guard it with our lives. It must not reach the sorcerer's clutches, and yet we need it on that forbidden mountain.'

Then, striking the Wand of Faith on the floor, Hope and Rielle were gone.

...

Wistfully, Far gazed outside. Sometimes, on a happy day, Flightlord, the rainbow dragon, would visit for a while to chat with her through a slither of open window. The rest of the time, Far did indeed mind Hope's room and guard the sixteenth door. It would not do to let the world, and Wish, know that Hope was far away. There were too many secrets, and too much precious knowledge stored in this part of the tower. Often, Far would flit to the sixteenth door and check that it was shut tight. Of course, it always was, but Far would still sigh with relief each time. She wasn't sure what she would do if something went wrong, despite the fact Hope had placed his faith in her.

Huge pots boiled with no visible flame on the window sills. They were filled with thick, dark moat mud. It was well known that moat mud from the Tower of Dreams carried special powers of protection. Not even the Sorcerer of Great Contempt could get past moat mud at its best!

A dark shadow crossed the window. Startled, Far looked up. Two huge yellow eyes peered in as a mist of hot air clouded the pane.

Happily, Far flew to the window. Squeezing through the open crack, she joined Flightlord the dragon, in the beauty of the morning. That was as far as she would ever dare to go; Hope's room was a sacred trust.

'Good morning,' Flightlord grinned, and the grin made him less formidable. Far settled, as always, upon his nose; it made him cross-eyed, but that was the fun of it.

'Any news?' Flightlord whispered, testing the landscape with blazing eyes.

Far shook her head. 'No,' she breathed, 'no news as yet.'
Was no news, good news? Or was it bad?

Silently, they contemplated the thought, but as they sat in agreeable companionship, a dark shadow crossed the bright blue sky. They looked up.

Greenish-black clouds scudded, like lost hurtling waves set free from a faraway ocean. A stray wind began to whip the little moat, forcing it to collide with the tower walls in an argument of stone and water. Thunder roared somewhere, but no lightning or rain followed. In a torment of wild blows, the clouds joined together until the entire mass became a dark, brooding shroud.

With eyes honed to sharp pins, Flightlord crouched with anticipation at something he could only sense.

'Go inside,' he whispered urgently to Far, 'and don't leave Hope's room. Something is happening that I don't understand.'

Far did as she was told, and then promptly pressed her face hard against the pane. Outside, clouds bubbled and bunched as if trapped and trying to escape some horror.

Flightlord sniffed the thickening air as he watched the clouds degrading. Wish grew gloomier as he did so, and then, the sun disappeared, plunging Wish into the deepest darkness that Flightlord had ever known.

Silence seeped through the air like a dank falsehood. Not a bird or creature stirred. With a flare of intensity, the giant pots of boiling moat mud on Hope's window ledges boiled furiously with renewed heat and protective power.

In all the years Flightlord had been visiting Wish, he had never seen anything to equal this. With the cunning of a rainbow dragon, he prepared for the worst. Sinister moments ticked by.

Was it a wish? Was it a stray thought, or were many humans wishing terrible things at once? After all, Wish did exist from the minds of humans.

But then, in a moment that took Flightlord's breath away, he understood. This was not the doing of any human! Even as the realisation hit home, something hard and brutal slammed him, sending him crashing to the ground.

Flightlord gasped. This was new to him. He had never encountered anything that dared attack a dragon! Furiously, with lightning speed, he recovered. Lashing his tail and flaring his nostrils, he prepared to spit a gush of flame.

Shrill laughter filled the air.

Far buzzed frantically. Hope's room groaned and shook. Wide-eyed with disbelief, Far turned and faced the back of the chamber. Something was at the sixteenth door! Far held her breath. Nothing could enter the sixteenth door. It was impossible. Nothing and no one could enter Hope's room unless they were invited!

Outside, the darkness was a ruinous mass of thick, congealed air that blocked Flightlord's breathing. Again, he was hit by a terrible force. Surprising himself, he moaned with pain. Cruel laughter shrilled, once again.

Flightlord knew what he had to do. Turning from the window, he raced to the entrance of the tower and burst inside. Reaching Hope's common doorway, he called out.

'Far, you must let me in!'

Far heard the call. It sounded like Flightlord, but Hope had ordered that neither of the doors to his room be unsealed. She peered through the common door's peep-hole. It *was* Flightlord! *What was she to do?* Hope had strictly warned her to keep the common door sealed. Unlike the sixteenth door, it was known to many and almost anyone could sneak in that way.

'Far, let me in!' Flightlord persisted.

Far jumped. Something was now rattling the walls!

'Think,' Far whispered, 'think.'

Settling herself onto a pile of Hope's beloved books, written by his hand and bound with devotion, she crouched carefully, placing her wings quietly by her side, the way she had been taught. The world outside the window darkened, even as her trusted friend begged her to let him in.

Closing her eyes, she settled her mind. Clearly, and as powerfully as she could, she thought of her mentor. Almost immediately she began to see him.

...

Hope stood on a jagged strip of rock. He held the Wand of

Faith in such a way that it beamed healing blue light. Far had seen that blue light, often.

Reaching further into her mind, and outward toward the First One, Far worked to see who he was trying to heal.

The herd surrounded something. White light from the Ritual of Return poured from the unicorns. Their faces were rigid and raw.

Far strove to see the shape on the ground.

A portion of Rielle's cloak came into view. Rielle! Was it Rielle who was hurt? Pud stood fixed, with a grin on his face.

Far looked again.

That was no grin! Pud was growling and looked ready to leap.

Far panicked, then settled, taking deep breaths.

Little Bobs stood to one side. Tears rolled down his sweet, young face.

Far became chilled. Reluctantly, she sent her mind to look further.

Oobaat held the Staff of Life in both hands, like an offering. His face wore the look of a First One in peril.

Cold realisation struck at Far's heart.

Rielle was crouched over something, a look of grim pleading on her face.

Far pushed further.

The shape was white.

Far flinched and recoiled.

Benny! A wound in his neck gaped open and raw. He was not breathing!

With a cry, Far opened her eyes.

The Ritual of Return was broken!

...

'Let me in!' Flightlord bellowed. 'Far, let me in!'

Terror flooded through the butterfly. She knew that the Sorcerer of Great Contempt could never enter the tower, but she also knew that in that moment, despite all that was true, he was trying!

Dashing with a crazed decision, Far spoke the words to unlock the common door, and Flightlord careered inside. Instantly, the door slammed shut and sealed itself again. In the farthest corner, the wall of the sixteenth door creaked and groaned.

Far and Flightlord looked at each other by the light of power that always drifted in Hope's room. The dragon took a deep, shuddering breath.

Far looked carefully at him and gasped. He was wounded! She took a closer look. He was bleeding! In all her life, and the years were considerable, she had never known a rainbow dragon to bleed.

'You've come to the right place,' she whispered in a frightened, tight voice. 'I'm sure there's a potion here somewhere, that will heal that gash on your side.'

'I've never been helpless before,' Flightlord gasped. 'I've never known what it meant.'

The dragon and the butterfly gazed at each other, while outside in Wish, the world went mad.

CHAPTER 10

That ridiculous hat

Bibs could not believe his eyes. One minute the herd were there and then next, they were gone! Puzzled, he looked anxiously around, but he was definitely alone. How could they just leave, and forget him like that? Any minute now, they would surely return. He resigned himself to wait.

He found a quiet, shady spot away from the blistering sun and cautiously nibbled on some old, drying leaves. He was worried about little Bobs, but the younger snail would soon come back at a snapping pace to grin cheekily, with a full belly, and a tall tale about the leaf he'd claimed… wouldn't he?

Bibs waited, but time went by and there was no sign of anyone. The sun was steadily climbing through the sky and the day was getting older. Worried, he wondered what to do next. Should he stay in case they all returned, or should he go and look for them? Perhaps Will would come back soon, and then they could go and find the others. Bibs waited, dozed, and finally snoozed.

Waking with a sharp snap, he felt a tug inside his

heart. Instinctively, he knew with all certainty that everything was wrong. No one had returned! Not little Bobs, or Will, or the herd. His heart chilled. What if no one ever returned?

He looked around and called out, but only a warm breeze rustled. Despite his better judgement, he decided to try and find them. Nothing moved, and the sun beamed leadenly down on him.

Alone on the mountain, his head reeled as unwanted thoughts leeched his courage. He pushed the thoughts away but they kept coming back until he knew he had to face them.

What if he went searching but never found anyone? What would he do? Could he find his way back to the forest? It was a very, very long way away. It had taken months to climb the mountain, but perhaps alone and unnoticed by the sorcerer, might he travel faster? He really needed to find little Bobs, though. It was his fault, after all, that little Bobs had come along on this strange and frightening journey. Bibs knew he would not rest until he was sure his young cousin had returned safely home. He had to find the others; there was no other way.

Trying hard not to be glum, Bibs cruised over rocks and beneath rotting logs. Surely, there would be tracks. As he slid, he saw something through the corner of an eye. Cautiously, he slowed and went toward it. Could it be? He gasped and sped up. Will's hat! The feather in the brim fluttered sadly, flickering almost eerily in the silent breeze. Bibs knew one thing for sure: Will went nowhere without his hat!

Glancing warily around, Bibs' heart lurched. The cliff

was broken, as surely as if someone had sliced it with an axe! Sick with dread, Bibs slid reluctantly to the brittle edge. Sure enough, imprints on the ground showed that Will had been there. Bibs went as close to the edge as he dared, doing his best to peer over it. The valley floor far, far below showed him nothing and gave no answers.

Heartsick, he turned back to the hat. It lay as sad proof of what must have happened to Will. Bibs felt bad about leaving it, despite it being a silly object. No one had ever wanted to tell Will how ridiculous it looked on him, and now they wouldn't have to.

Close by, a rock ledge made an overhang. Grasping the hat in his mouth, Bibs dragged it with much grunting and grumbling, and finally settled it to rest under the ledge. It would stay dry there, at least for a while, as a sort of monument to Will's memory. Bibs felt it was the least he could do.

With a small salute to Will, and a tear in his eye for the human he had barely known, Bibs finally moved away. He looked back at the hat one last time, and sighed sadly as the feather in its brim waved gently in the breeze.

Bibs continued, less sure now of anything. Had the unicorns gone looking for Will? Did they know how he had met his end? If so, why hadn't they taken him, Bibs, with them? Ever since they had begun this journey, the unicorns and the First Ones had sheltered the snails. Why would that change now? Bibs knew one thing: it must be bad indeed if they had left so quickly that he had been forgotten. His heart plunged. He cast his mind back to the climb so far. It had been a hard, cruel journey filled with dangerous surprises sent by the sorcerer to torment them.

Sliding cautiously, Bibs remembered parts of the past months as if their burden might never go away. He shook his head with dismay. The team had stuck together, until now! Bibs thought longingly of the forest. It was safe there, for all of them. He flinched at a passing cloud, but it was just a cloud.

Disillusioned and tired, Bibs paused beneath a stumpy bush. A shadow blocked the sun. Looking up, Bibs cringed. With avid strokes from its powerful wings, an eagle, russet and bronze, called with cries of yearning as it cruised the currents of the wind. Casually, as if it were the master of all time, it embraced the sky with piercing eyes and then, calling once more, it went away. Something stirred inside Bibs like a distant memory, but he couldn't grasp what it was. Shaking his head, he looked skyward. Sure that all was clear, he slid on.

In a rush and flurry of wings, Bibs saw huge claws flash toward him, but too late, the eagle had clutched him in its massive talons. Bibs hid inside his shell, but what good would that do him now? The eagle, it seemed, had sealed his fate.

CHAPTER 11

When days of youth and glory fall

Benny looked up. He was back in the forest! Beloved, ancient, time-grown trees reared above his head. Spreading their canopy from branch to branch, they joined each other in a comfortable cathedral, murmuring in gentle voices to the wind. Mosses that smelled of rich dark earth squished invitingly under Benny's feet. He inhaled the glory of the forest. Tossing his heels in a revelation of joy, Benny galloped, pranced and bucked as if he were a foal. Sliding to a stop and snorting loudly, he challenged the very air to play. Butterflies drifted in happy pairs as a brook gurgled and played over rocks. Golden light wavered as the sun begged entrance to the deep of the forest.

Benny gazed around for the herd. They would be here somewhere. With a happy spring to his step he trotted off, trilling. They trilled back. With a leap, he galloped to join them as they called his name again and again.

...

Rielle had not taken her hand from Benny's still body. Dry eyed, she repeated his name over and over, as if doing so could bring him back.

'Benny,' she whispered, 'Benny.' It had become a litany that she was barely aware of.

Time passed. *Too much time*. The Ritual of Return had been broken for precious minutes, but it was too soon for Rielle to think about that now. She was focused on one thing only and that was her beloved unicorn friend. The wound in Benny's neck pulsed as the herd and First Ones worked with all their skill to rid the evil poison that lurked within him.

Candela, Coraggio, Oobaat and Hope glanced meaningfully at each other as they made their healing. If the journey up the mountain had been hard before this, then now, it could be impossible. Neves On, they knew, might well be free. After all of this time, he had succeeded in breaking the Ritual of Return. Grave danger faced them now! With a renewed burst of effort, the herd and First Ones used their skill to bring Benny back. Above, an eagle called, breaking the silence. The sound was sad, solemn and enquiring.

In a moment that none of them would ever forget, Benny suddenly plunged to his feet. Gasping with life, he stood, quivering and wide-eyed. In the next moment the wound in his neck closed over, as if it had never been.

Rielle leapt to her own feet. *Benny was different. Something was different!* She looked enquiringly at the herd. Their eyes were sharp pin-pricks. The First Ones, too, stood silently by, watching the little unicorn thoughtfully and offering no greeting. Rielle frowned, surprised. Why didn't anyone speak?

Pud still scanned the landscape with angry, amber

eyes, while little Bobs continued to sit apart and alone.

And then it happened. Benny began to change. *He begañ to grow.*

Bewildered, Rielle watched the faces of the First Ones, but their expressions gave nothing away.

Benny grew in front of everyone's eyes until he was as large as Coraggio. For the first time ever at equal height, father and son stared eye to eye.

The herd sighed with relief then, and the First Ones went forward to greet Benny joyously, as if he had returned from a very long journey.

At last, Candela stepped up to her son. 'Benemerito,' she murmured, 'you've returned to us in the outside world.'

Benny looked deeply into his mother's eyes. 'I've grown up, haven't I?' he asked calmly.

'You have, son,' Candela replied. 'The herd is now complete.'

Rielle stood by, dumfounded. Was there no end to the strange goings on? Why in blazes had little Benny, on the point of death, grown from being small, to being as tall as the rest of the herd? She didn't understand. She had always assumed he was meant to be a little unicorn, but now this!

Benny peered around as if reacquainting himself with the world. His gaze fell on Rielle. She noticed that his eyes glowed with something that hadn't been there before. He winked at her. Rielle rushed forward in a surge of relief, throwing her arms around his large, silken neck.

'I prayed so hard for you!' she called, before breaking into sobs.

'There, there,' Benny crooned, 'I'm alive and well, and all grown up, as you can see.'

Rielle stood back, relieved, even as realisation hit her. She turned to the First Ones.

'The Ritual of Return was broken, wasn't it?' she whispered.

Hope and Oobaat simply nodded.

Rielle turned and faced Candela and Coraggio. '*He* escaped, didn't he?'

'Yes,' Coraggio nodded wryly, 'I'm afraid Neves On, Number Seven of the First Ones, the *Sorcerer of Great Contempt*, could well be free.'

'What will it mean?' Rielle insisted. 'How will we know what to do now?'

Oobaat placed a steady hand on her shoulder. 'In the face of evil,' he replied quietly, 'we stay calm.'

Rielle looked up at him. His face was kind and comforting. She took a deep breath. 'But he has the Staff of the Unimaginable,' she breathed. 'How can we possibly reach Old's caves with his power blocking and probably stalking us on our way?'

How much more could they all take?

Oobaat took his hand from her shoulder. Not replying, he strode away some paces. For several minutes, he remained staring at something only he could see. Rielle waited, heartsick and stricken, her eyes haunted from the horrors of the morning. Oobaat turned at last to look at her. He sighed.

'Gold,' he finally replied in a hushed voice that he hoped only the group could hear, 'gold is what he seeks now.'

Rielle shook her head, puzzled. She could feel Old's golden cake tin where she carried it close to her hip. She didn't fully understand all this fuss about gold.

Oobaat nodded as if to a silent question.

'Eerht Ytnewt On, Number Twenty Three of the First Ones, or as you called him Rielle, *Old...* had learned that patience is the stepping stone of wise men and that being humble is the key to great things.'

Rielle nodded. Her throat grew tight. Yes, Old had been kind and wise, and humble and patient. Old had changed her forever, deep inside her heart.

Oobaat took a step closer to the herd and Rielle.

'Old knew how to do the work, you see. He spent long, lonely years perfecting his purpose and now, well, now, Neves On would like to steal that, and try to capture the essence of it, to be his own.'

Oobaat's usually warm eyes glittered. 'Number Seven has proven he is a thief. He thought nothing of stealing the unicorn wand. *The unicorn wand!* What brazen madness! So, why would he baulk at stealing the gold of time?' He peered pointedly at Rielle, as if entreating her to understand. 'Longevity; Neves On seeks to steal the gold that Old made, and learn the secrets to eternal life.'

The herd shuddered.

Perplexed, Rielle looked entreatingly at the unicorns.

'Nothing ever lasts forever, but nothing ever ends,' Rielle muttered under her breath. 'That's what the eagle said. You know... the one who was there after he... after Old... died.' She frowned. 'If Old knew the secret of living forever, then why did he leave us? Why did he...

die?' She finished the question in a strangled whisper.

'Don't distress yourself,' Candela urged. 'The explosion tore through Old's body and damaged it too much. Not even the Ritual of Return could mend it, so he chose to leave it and go away. But,' her eyes twinkled in a cryptic look, 'without change, Rielle, there would be no purpose.'

Rielle glanced at Hope and then Oobaat, as if trying to understand something more.

'What do you mean by the gold he *made?* Doesn't gold make itself?'

Oobaat smiled bafflingly. 'Number twenty three studied the secrets of earth and air and stardust; he earned the right to live forever. But Neves On wants to steal those secrets without doing *any* of the work. Now do you understand?'

Rielle still wanted to know more, but the herd tensed, ears pricked. Hope and Oobaat glared alertly, and Pud bristled with renewed fire.

'Come,' Oobaat whispered, 'we must move on.' He glanced at Coraggio. 'Where's Will?' he muttered urgently. 'Why isn't he here?'

Little Bobs could not stay silent any longer. 'Bibs is missing too!' he cried.

Pud nudged him to stifle his shrillness. Loud noises echoed on the mountain and they had to be quiet to survive.

The herd and the First Ones looked pointedly at each other.

'Will and Bibs are missing?' asked Benny. 'You were preoccupied with me, and somehow they got lost?'

'It has begun then,' Hope growled. 'Separation is the one thing we cannot afford. It's dangerous for us all.' He frowned.

'Will was behind me in the fog,' Coraggio interrupted, 'but he must have chosen not to follow.' He shook his head. 'The boy has too much conceit!'

'What about Bibs though?' little Bobs asked sadly. 'Shouldn't he have been with the herd?'

'Yes, he should have come with us as part of our group,' Candela gasped, surprised. 'I don't understand why he isn't here. He always stayed close.'

Candela and Coraggio looked puzzled.

'He wasn't close,' little Bobs whispered into the small silence that followed. 'We were… we were, well, chasing a big, juicy leaf.'

Everyone stared at little Bobs. He blushed and hung his head.

'Oh,' Candela nodded, 'I see, then he must have been outside of our circle of light when we left in haste.' She paused, concerned. 'We must go back immediately and find Bibs and Will.'

'Let's hurry,' Coraggio urged, 'if we hurry we might still find them safe and well.'

The words had barely left his mouth when the sky above them erupted, showering them with brutal lashings of ice and water.

CHAPTER 12

Creatures of flight in dire plight

In the Tower of Dreams, things were not as they should have been, while outside in Wish, the sky broiled in such dark, brooding, black-green corruption that it was impossible to see anything at all.

Flightlord staggered into Hope's room, gasping, before falling leadenly to the floor. Far gaped, goggle eyed. This couldn't be! Nothing could harm a rainbow dragon. Dragons weren't governed by the laws of Wish, they were powerful creatures that rode the wind and disappeared to a land and laws of their own making. How could this happen? For a terrifying moment, Far felt such doubt that her world spun and her head reeled. *Was the tower still safe? Would the sixteenth door be broken? Would the secrets of Hope's room be kept? Could Hope's potions fix Flightlord?*

Flightlord lay panting unevenly, his powerful face and jaws slackened, with his eyes rolling from side to side.

Trying not to panic, and ignoring the force rattling the sixteenth door, Far began reading labels on the many bottles of coloured potions that Hope used to cure ills and ailments. Had Hope ever needed to cure a dragon? Far doubted it, so what might work?

Shelves filled with colourful cures and concoctions reached from floor to ceiling. Far grunted; the Tower of Dreams had such high ceilings and there was so much to choose from. Minutes went by and Far despaired. She tried to settle her mind, but whatever threatened from outside kept beating thunderously against the secret door, making her lose her place and forcing her to start again. Finally, she realised she was getting nowhere. She took a quick look at Flightlord. His eyes were closed but he was still breathing, if a little strangely. She hovered to one of his ears, frowning.

'Flightlord!' she bellowed. He didn't move. 'Flightlord, you can't die!' she roared, as loudly as she could.

Flightlord opened one eye and blinked. 'You... don't have to scream,' he panted, 'I'm... wounded... not deaf.'

Joyously, Far smacked him as hard as she could with one wing and grinned in delight at his strangled reply.

'Good,' she squealed, 'don't move, alright? I'm looking for something to make your wound go away!'

Flightlord grunted and closed his eye. *Don't move? If he could move he would not be lying helpless and mortified, on Hope's floor!* He grunted again. As unusual as this situation was, the little butterfly and her bellowing made it feel as if things were almost normal.

He sighed in resignation and lay there, bemused. He had never heard of a rainbow dragon being cut down before, although there was that time he remembered, long, long ago, when Candela had saved his life. He recalled it as if it were yesterday. Despite his current unfortunate situation, Flightlord smiled to himself.

He had been very young and Wish had been so beautiful that day. He had been too caught up in the joy of living to watch what he was doing.

'Silly young thing that I was,' he grinned, 'and what a wonderful way to meet a unicorn for the first time.'

Far looked down and panicked. Flightlord was grimacing from ear to ear and making garbled sounds! She must hurry and find a cure. Her friend was obviously in unbearable agony!

Flightlord chuckled at his memories.

He had just been taught how to fly and in a wonderful moment of freedom and power, he had left the other rainbow dragons and gone off alone for the first time.

Discovering the joys of rolling through the sky, he had soared, but since it was new to him, he missed his landing mark and plummeted headfirst into a large blue lake. He couldn't believe it. He had just kept sinking deeper and deeper, until at last he touched the bottom.

Flightlord chortled.

He clearly remembered the moment of panic he had felt when he found himself sitting, watching fish go by. He had tried to go back up, but something was wrong. He hadn't been able to move!

Far looked down and panicked even more. Now Flightlord was hallucinating and choking, by the sounds of it!

Flightlord was enjoying his memories. It took his mind from the fact that for the first time in his life he was forced to be still.

Sitting there on the bottom of the lake, he had tried to take a breath, discovering that when he did so, his nose and mouth filled with water and it made him cough and gag. That had absolutely made it worse! Soon he was swallowing water and breathing it in and coughing and then choking and running out of air. He flapped his wings but they were useless. Then it had happened, a moment he would never forget, when his whole world changed and would never be the same again.

In a beam of bright light, a lovely white head had pushed through the water and called him gently by his name. He had looked up. A creature of amazing beauty looked back. Her eyes met his in that fateful moment and he had been drawn to her velvet gaze.

'Come Flightlord,' she had smiled, 'you can do it! Swim, and then you'll soon be flying again.'

Believing her with all his heart, Flightlord, the infant rainbow dragon, lifted from the lake floor, and had begun to swim. In just a few moments he had leapt clear of the water and was flying again!

The creature had gazed up at him. 'You see,' she had beamed, 'today you learned how to fly, and also how to swim!'

'Who are you?' he had squeaked, romping happily after his near miss. 'Who are you? I have never seen anyone like you before!'

The creature had laughed merrily. 'Candela,' she had trilled, 'I am Candela!'

Blinking, she shook water from her long mane and white body to send spray flying in silver droplets, everywhere.

Flightlord had hovered. 'What are you, Candela?' he had queried, with the open curiosity of the very young.

She was trotting away, but over her shoulder she had called out. 'I am a Lilifel, or as some would say, a unicorn.' Then, in a race of joy, she had flung up her heels and galloped with all her power and swiftness toward the Valley of Possibility and the Tower of Dreams. Soon she was far away. Flightlord was left to hover, spellbound by her charm.

'I owe you my life, Lilifel,' he had whispered, watching the speck she had become, 'and for you and your kind, I will always be of service if you should ever need me.'

Flightlord blinked moistly at the memory then made a happy sound.

Far looked down from where she was perched and held back a frantic squeal. Now Flightlord was moaning and groaning! Feverishly, she scanned potions until at last she saw something she thought might work. It was a bottle of purple liquid. The label read: <u>For Creatures of Cold Blood.</u>

Far paused and wondered. Dragons were just giant lizards with wings, weren't they? Then Flightlord must have cold blood! Perfect, but how to move the bottle from all the way up there, to where he was lying on the floor? Far flapped around in circles; there were times when she would prefer to be something other than a butterfly, perhaps something big with hands and feet.

'Think,' she scolded herself, 'think!' In a lightning moment, she knew what to do. Flying with all her might, she nose-dived to the dragon and, landing on his face, bit him on the nose.

Flightlord had been having a nice nap. 'Far,' he bellowed, 'what is it now?'

'I've got it,' Far yelped proudly, 'I've found something that might work!'

Flightlord opened an eye. 'Where? What? Hmm?' he sighed.

'Wait, just wait, I'll send it down to you,' she cried.

Racing for time and doing the best that she knew how, Far flew with all speed back to the purple potion. Grunting with the effort, she tugged at the lid. It was tightly pushed on. She tugged and pulled and finally, in an enormous jerk, she lifted the lid from the jar. She looked down. Fortunately, Flightlord was looking up. With a mighty shove, Far pushed the jar with all her strength.

'Open your mouth!' she roared.

Too alarmed to disobey, Flightlord did as he was told. The jar tipped as it fell, and as luck would have it, large amounts of the potion flowed nicely into his mouth. Flightlord made a face. It tasted horrible. He gulped and swallowed, just before the jar hit him on the head. But Far didn't notice. Grinning from ear to ear, she sat on his nose until Flightlord went cross-eyed, just the way she liked.

'You see,' Far chirped, 'I told you I was born under a lucky star!'

Just then the world outside went quiet, and whatever had been banging on the sixteenth door went away, and left them alone.

CHAPTER 13

Falling felt good for a while
But then I landed and lost my smile

As distrustful as Will was of the eagle, a part of him wanted it to stay. A corner of his mind reasoned that if it hadn't hurt him so far, then perhaps it never would. Reluctantly, he admitted to himself that the creature was company of sorts, and anything was better than being alone on the ledge. Besides, the night was bitter on that bare, solitary spot, and the eagle sheltered him a little from biting winds.

As the night rolled on, Will felt his eyelids droop. Curled into a tight ball with his knees pulled close to his chest, and holding the Wand of Time tightly, he lay down and placed a hand under his head as a makeshift pillow. Despite misgivings, hunger and thirst, his eyelids closed, and at last, he slept.

Will stirred in the deep of night to the sound of rain, and wondered why he was not getting wet. His fogged brain knew he was still on the misbegotten ledge, but dazed, he couldn't grasp why he was dry. He tried to sit up but something large was held a hand's breadth above him. Baffled, he reached out with timid fingers and, surprisingly, felt the downy smoothness of feathers. Bemused, he realised the eagle was holding a wing outstretched to cover him. He fell back into profound sleep. Rain continued through the long, dreary darkness, as Will slumbered beneath the eagle's shelter.

It was daylight when Will awoke after what seemed like a night of dreams filled with work. The eagle wasn't there. Will sat up. The wall behind him dripped, and beside him there were puddles to remind him of the rain. The valley below was a wonderland of green.

Was this ledge where the eagle lived? If so, why did it tolerate him being there, and why had it kept him dry?

Will glanced down. Beside him, there was a pile of berries. He frowned, contemplating them. Surely only the bird could have put them there. He couldn't take his eyes off the ripe, juicy fruit. His mouth watered unbearably. He wanted to grab them and gulp them down, but what would he do if the bird returned and wanted the berries for itself? It might peck at him, or worse.

Chill, easterly winds blustered around the mountainside in playful spurts. Will shivered. He probed around in his mind for ways to leave the ledge, but there were no answers. His stomach growled and his parched lips hurt. Desolate, he shut his eyes.

What a way for his life to end! He had wanted to go home… was that so bad?

Leaning back onto the wall of the mountain, Will fought moments of dizziness. Tears battled to sit on his heart, and his throat ached with despair. He opened his eyes and gazed at the endless sunlit blue sky. It was very beautiful. Maybe it would be just as easy to drop from the ledge after all. Perhaps that was his fate.

He held the wand to his cheek, and she sang.

Willful James note your might
Keep despair from your heart
Sorrow masks the truth of time
Sorrow rules from dark not light

Let no darkness
Break the core
Of the boy
Called up by law

Let no evil win the day
Or steal from Wish and the world
Its frail ways
Of light and joy.

Will sighed and shut his eyes. The wand was giving him counsel that seemed hard to follow in that moment, but he held her tightly and with gratitude. She gave him solace he didn't deserve.

A sound made him open his eyes. The eagle had returned, and in its beak it held another cluster of berries. It placed the laden branch deliberately upon Will's lap, eyed him with its warm auburn eyes, then turned its back to sit at the farthest end of the ledge.

Will's heart leapt. Surely it was giving him a clear message. Despite his hunger and thirst, he paused. Did you thank a wild creature? Did you even try to speak to it? He cleared his throat. He felt foolish, yet his gratitude was so intense, he found he had to say something before he could eat.

'Thank you,' he whispered.

The eagle still sat looking away but briefly turned its head, blinked knowing eyes at Will, then looked away again. It squatted with such a proud bearing that Will marvelled that it was bothering with him.

Will's hand trembled as he picked up the branch. The first berry tasted so good it exploded moistly in his throat. He knew he should make them last, but he crammed the berries eagerly into his mouth. Shooting a quick look at the eagle's back, he also made short work of the ones next to him.

With all the fruit eaten, Will found he was breathing with effort, as if he had just been for a run. This latest adventure had made him weak.

He remembered the last time he had felt like this. But that time, Flightlord, the rainbow dragon, and Far, the butterfly, had rescued him and taken him to the Tower of Dreams, where Hope had saved his life. He remembered how suspicious of them he had been. He grimaced at his folly.

They weren't there to save him this time.

Will leaned back onto the mountain and shut his eyes again. For a terrible moment he missed them all with such longing that he felt it would choke him. Red berry juice had dripped from his chin to his clothes and onto the wand, but he didn't care.

Sighing deeply, he whispered aloud. 'How do I get off this ledge? How can I ever leave?'

The wand chanted softly.

Let go of attachment
And all will be revealed

Will didn't understand. Frowning, he opened his eyes. To his surprise, the eagle had come to sit beside him. Its warm, soft feathers brushed his arm with unexpected firmness.

Louder than before, the Wand of Time repeated her words.

Let go of attachment
And all will be revealed

'What attachment?' Will breathed. 'What do you mean?'

The eagle turned to look at him as if perhaps Will was speaking to it. Its bold eyes bored into Will's, and its beak looked fierce and frighteningly large. It sat so closely that Will felt each breath it took.

The eagle stood. From where Will sat, the creature was enormous. Without warning, and in a movement both lightning fast and terrifyingly hard, it barged with all its might into Will.

Gasping with disbelief, Will had no time to think. Clutching the Wand of Time firmly as if she were a part of him, he watched himself from the outside in, as his body lost its place on the ledge.

Once again, to his horror, Will began to fall. He made one clumsy attempt to remain on the ledge, but it was just a slab of slippery rock and gave him no handhold. He fell.

This time, the sky appeared to embrace him in its wide blue arms as if it were his dear friend, and not an unusual place to be. With what presence of mind and strength he had, Will clutched the wand in both arms and fiercely shut his eyes. The wand sang for him.

Let go of attachment
And all will be revealed

Freezing winds whipped Will and his stomach lurched, but he knew there was no point in fighting. Resigned, he no longer feared what would be his end. He heard a sound and opened his eyes. The eagle was gliding beside him as if Will, too, had wings. Once again the eagle stared boldly at him, and again, it lurched into Will with all the power at its command.

Will was shoved into the wall of the mountain, his bones jarring with the thud. The eagle rushed him again, and this time, from the mighty push, Will became jammed into a gap in the mountain wall. Winded, he held his breath and waited for the next mighty shove, but it never came.

Holding the wand safely in one hand, he caught his breath. Astonishingly, he was standing on something solid! He looked up. The eagle swooped and hovered close by for moments more, and then, with a triumphant call, it disappeared from sight.

Will didn't dare look down. He shut his eyes, and this time, he kept them closed.

Oh shock of power

Beneath the deluge of rain that poured with a fiery thirst upon them, the unicorns, Rielle, Pud and little Bobs bunched together as best they could, huddled into a corner of mountain that barely gave them shelter.

Icy water pounded them for the better part of half the day until they thought it was never going to go away. Freezing winds whipped and flailed the manes and tails of the unicorns until they looked like foam on ocean waves.

Little Bobs hid and snuggled beneath Pud, who hid and snuggled beneath Benny, as Rielle hid and snuggled beneath the mass of unicorn bodies. Oobaat and Hope, however, stood tall in the rain, their faces turned toward the oncoming deluge as they held a private, silent vigil. With their wands held high for much of the time, they appeared unaffected.

Watching the First Ones from her makeshift shelter, Rielle sensed they were hard at work. Even despite huddling beneath the unicorns, she was sodden. She looked to where her own blood had soaked her that morning, and saw it was one less thing she would need to worry about; the rain had washed her tunic clean.

Although they were drenched, the warmth from the unicorn herd carried itself to everyone there. White light flowed over all of them, keeping them snug enough to cope, and protecting them from the perilous cold. Then, just as suddenly as it had begun, the rain and ice stopped. With swift justice, the searing sun poured back up the mountainside, quickly drying everything in its path.

Soon the travellers, too, were dry. Although they were familiar with the mountain running hot and cold, and also with its difficult and mysterious moods, it was impossible to become accustomed to it. In some ways the mountain reminded Rielle of Will.

Oobaat and Hope kept their silent vigil for a while longer, as if they were completing a task that only they understood. The herd and the others waited patiently. At last, the First Ones stirred.

'We must go back for Will and Bibs,' Coraggio stated, stepping forward. 'We cannot risk them being separated from us for much longer.' He turned and looked at everyone there. 'Are we ready?'

The herd, First Ones, Rielle, Pud and little Bobs were caught in the power of the Ritual of Return. They found themselves standing where Bibs had been left behind.

Candela turned to little Bobs. 'Is this exactly where you and Bibs were?'

Little Bobs nodded, round-eyed. Candela smiled kindly at the unhappy young snail.

'Spread out, but don't separate,' Candela trilled to the

others. Pausing, her gaze fell on Rielle. 'We cannot lose anyone else,' she whispered.

The Ritual of Return had been broken. From now on, it was something they must never forget. Nothing would ever be the same, and it must never happen again.

They steered clear of large rocks and shrubs. There was no room for error or mishaps now. It would not do to meet another hidden wolf with poison in its fangs. Snorting warily, the herd spread out.

Rielle clutched the bump in her travel sack where Old's cake tin rested by her side. Hope threw her a look of caution. Rielle stopped fidgeting.

The First Ones had considered long and hard about who should carry Old's golden cake tin up the mountain. After much discussion, they had decided to allow Rielle to mind the precious item. From it came their one source of food. Most importantly, it was dangerously made from Old's gold. They knew that the sorcerer would easily assume that anything made of gold would be carefully guarded by his brothers. Despite Hope and Oobaat arguing the risk, Rielle had insisted on the ruse. Danger stalked them constantly, but Rielle was prepared now, as fate had chosen, to fight for what was right and good, on pain of death if need be, as that morning had proven.

Oobaat and Hope walked on either side of Rielle, as Pud stalked carefully behind her with a broken pace that kept him glaring, turning and baring his lips in constant soft growls. Little Bobs clung to Candela's side, careful not to get in her way, yet determined not to be left behind like poor Bibs. Despite the recent attack and his deathly experience, Benny walked in front, flanked by wary members of the herd.

Rielle studied Benny. His new height and stature suited him. A memory flashed through her mind. She saw him as he had been that distant morning when they had first met, in the green and gold of the protected forest. Sadness tugged her. Nothing would ever be quite the same again. Benny the little unicorn was no more. Her memory stirred. What was it she had heard that fateful morning when they had lost Old? *Nothing ever lasts forever, but nothing ever ends.* That was it.

Rielle sighed. He was still her Benny, the Benny who had poured himself into her untrusting heart and changed her life forever. He was still her dear, treasured friend. But he *was* different, as everything was now. She frowned. For all they knew, the sorcerer could be free and watching them that very moment.

All eyes scoured the landscape, doing their best to miss nothing. They could not be sure when or if the sorcerer would discover them, even though unicorn light pulsed around them for protection, as best as it could.

Abruptly, Benny stopped. He pawed at the ground, tossing his head urgently, his eyes ablaze. Merging swiftly forward, the herd went to him. No one spoke. The mountain shuddered and fluffed itself, and then sat still.

Rielle walked quickly to the huddled herd, and reaching them, she gasped at what she saw. Will's hat slumped wetly, partly hidden by a small rock ledge. Rielle stifled a cry and glanced around for Will.

Hope held a finger to his lips.

Rielle looked at the hat again. The feather was soggy from the recent rain and almost completely tattered and torn. Swift tears rushed her eyes. She searched the landscape, just in case, but of course, Will wasn't there. She locked eyes with Oobaat. She knew what he was thinking. It was what everyone was thinking. Will did not go anywhere without his ridiculous hat!

After several moments, Hope leaned down to the muddy ground and picked up the hat. He looked carefully at it, as if hoping it might give him a clue to the whereabouts of its owner. He frowned and examined the brim. Tiny marks dented it. He passed the hat to Oobaat and pointed at the dents. Oobaat nodded and held the hat for both Coraggio and Candela to see. Candela frowned. The First Ones and the unicorns could see that the dents were made by Bibs. Had Will and Bibs been together?

Above them, an eagle shrieked. They all looked up at the closeness of its call. The eagle hovered near the cliff edge, swooping several times before it flew away. Heeding the warning, Benny walked with delicate steps as closely to the edge as he thought was safe. Hope and Oobaat followed.

'There are tracks, slightly faded by the rain, but footprints... human footprints... and, some snail marks,' Benny stated, taking a deep breath.

The rest of the herd didn't dare to step on the fragile outcrop.

Rielle pushed her way to the front of the herd. The ledge that Will had stood on confronted them with its story. She felt sick. It was obvious by the torn turf and rocky debris that the cliff had snapped like brittle toffee.

She tiptoed as close to the edge as she dared. Nothing but blue sky greeted her as she tried to see where Will had fallen. A sob caught her throat, and despite her resolve not to make a sound, her heartbreak carried softly on the corners of the wind. Distraught, she back-stepped abruptly, not taking her eyes from the torn ledge. Carelessly, she bumped into Hope.

The sudden hard shove dislodged the Wand of Faith from Hope's hand, and with a swift movement and a gasp of apology, Rielle caught the wand before it hit the ground. A surge of power shocked through her, and in a moment that stole Rielle's breath away, the Wand of Faith began to sing.

CHAPTER 15

Greedy

Bibs cringed as the eagle clutched him in its massive talons. Hiding deeply in the confines of his shell, he hoped the shell would protect him.

Bibs knew he had let everyone down. There was no way now that he could make sure little Bobs ever got back to the forest. He lamented the day he had played his silly trick on Rana, the gatekeeper's helper, and then snuck himself and his cousin into Wish. He reminded himself to never play silly tricks again, but then realised that it looked as if he would never have the opportunity. His heart filled with dismay. The worst part was that he had dragged poor little Bobs with him on this perilous journey.

Icy winds rushed past as the eagle flew speedily through the sky that was its natural road. Bibs hoped they would fly for as long as possible so he would have time to think of a way to escape. At least that's what he told himself, as he tried not to dwell on what was surely going to be his grisly end.

The eagle called, a powerful cry that mastered its domain, and the sound boomed inside Bibs' shell.

How would the others cope, not knowing where he was? He was nothing but a nuisance! They would search for him and waste precious time when they should be searching for Old's gold instead! And Will... would they find Will? Surely if they discovered what had happened to Will, that would dismay them more than losing a pesky snail... even one from the Imperial Guard?

In a moment of longing, Bibs imagined the forest as it had been on that last fateful morning, green and serene, his precious home. He could almost smell the moss and taste the juicy leaves. Leaves! It was because he was greedily chasing a leaf that he was now about to be eaten! He should have known better in this important fate-filled time, and not wandered away just because his stomach was calling.

Little Bobs... what had befallen him? He too had chased the leaf! Bibs cringed. Where had it taken him? If something terrible happened to little Bobs it would be Bibs' fault. Perhaps, Bibs brooded; he deserved to be eaten by the eagle. Perhaps it was some kind of payback for his bad deeds? He sighed. He had disobeyed Coraggio and had come to Wish, after being told not to, and he had done it for all the wrong reasons, in a fit of pettiness, to prove he was clever and right. It was meant to have been a joke, but it had sorely backfired. He resigned himself to his doom. Yes, perhaps the eagle taking him was a sign of justice, after all.

The eagle called again, and slowed.

Cowering, Bibs prepared. This was it, then! He would fight for as long as he could of course, but the eagle was enormous. Who could know how swiftly it would take that fearsome beak and those huge talons to make an end of him?

The eagled stopped, landed, and placed Bibs down.

Time went by. Bibs trembled harder with each passing moment. The waiting was the worst part. He almost preferred the eagle to just get on with it and not keep him in suspense. More time went by.

Bibs began to hear noises. He listened carefully. He could hear water trickling somewhere - a slow, steady sound that might have been soothing, in other circumstances.

He heard the eagle call again. Surprising him, the sound seemed distant, as if the call came from far away. What did it mean? Did he dare take a peek? Was it a ploy to force his head outside his shell so the eagle could promptly go in for the kill? That was silly; all the eagle had to do was crush his shell between beak and claws. A matter of moments was all it would take!

Without warning, the mountain briefly shook and boomed. Bibs was rolled and bumped ruthlessly around. Stopping, Bibs knew he had to take a chance. He poked his eyes over his shell's edge then caught his breath. The eagle was gone! He looked around curiously. It couldn't be true!

Why would the eagle have brought him here and left him? What was the meaning of it all?

Cautiously, Bibs began to slide around. He looked up, he looked down, and he looked from side to side. *Yes, this had to be it!* He stopped. *Why him? Why was he brought to this place?* A tear came to his eye. He was privileged indeed to be here. *Why him?*

A glow lit the air; a glow of gold.

Bibs sat then, inside Old's caves, and wondered, in that fateful moment, how he could let the others know, that he, Bibs, had already found what it was they were seeking.

CHAPTER 16

Not for me integrity

The Sorcerer of Great Contempt inhaled a great lungful of air in tremendous anticipation. Clutching the Staff of the Unimaginable in both hands carefully, he watched and waited. Like a longed-for apparition from the deepest parts of his mind, an aperture appeared from the very fabric of the atmosphere around him. The gap inched open.

A coruscating force of light burst through the opening with a blast that almost sent him flying. Holding his ground, Neves On stepped fiercely toward its beckoning. A dark grin spread on his features. With his eyes blazing, he squared his shoulders in a self-satisfied shrug. Wasting no more time, and with a wild cry, Number Seven of the First Ones strode through the cavity, as freedom flushed his wicked soul. The rupture slammed shut, leaving Wish behind!

A torrent of power pulled Neves On like a small, lost magnet through the void that separated Wish and the outside world. Crushed against the darkness of the void's walls, he smirked. The black, greasy emptiness was a thrill to his mind.

Not for him the wet ride of wishing ponds. Not for him the neat recording of his passing. Not for him, idle chit chat with solemn gatekeepers, those pious witnesses of all things right and properly done! This threshold, despite its unholy shadows, was his and his alone. It beckoned in a language he understood, reaching into his awareness, demanding a cry of victory, a call of triumph. At last he would end a thousand years of treachery; his banishment would be reckoned with.

Clutching at him from a source of power that was wrought for crucial moments from the devastation of the Ritual of Return, the darkness sucked into the secret parts of his being, leaving even him gasping at the lack of light.

To Neves On's bewilderment, fear, like a sleek sabre's blade, pierced him where his heart should have been, the heart he had stopped using, long, long ago. He clutched his chest and howled at the pain. Doing so, he almost dropped the Staff of the Unimaginable. Panic coursed pathetically through him. Such panic confounded him; surely, wasn't this only for weaklings and cowards?

Grasping the white wand nervously, he accidentally touched her scores. She burned him. Misery flushed his senses. How long would this passage take?

He had dreamed of this moment so many times and yet, not like this. He had imagined his escape from Wish to be filled with wonderful moments, perhaps of trumpets blaring and banners flying, but instead, the darkness gripped and pummelled persistently, blowing bolts of freezing air to afflict him.

Anger seethed in the sorcerer's belly at yet another injustice. He struggled within the void, but now that he was inside, it held him in a time and place all its own.

This should have been a greater moment!

As the blackness flung him like a straw, visions began to fill his mind. He saw the unicorn herd with his brothers. Neves On hissed. They were coursing white and blue light vigorously into the little unicorn, Benny. He hated Benny almost as much as he despised the she unicorn, Candela.

His trained wolf had done well to bring the little unicorn down.

'Hurry,' he screeched to the power that tugged him closer to his long-awaited destination. 'Hurry!'

He grimaced as a shock of pain closed over his mind, and once again, he saw the unicorn herd and his brothers. This time the vision showed the maimed unicorn moving. He saw the scene in every detail as if a giant magnifying glass were held to his eyes. First, the wound closed over, and then, the unicorn breathed.

'Hurry!' he roared, with such intensity that his lungs burned.

The vision played in front of him as surely as if the herd and the First Ones were there with him, inside his self-made place of travel, inside the capsule that hurled him farther and farther away from Wish.

Neves On panicked with renewed outrage. The vision revealed how the herd held vigil, their dark, velvet eyes filled with knowing and assurance.

'Hurry!' he gasped, as he watched Benny stand tall.

The void pulsed around him, hurling him and the Staff of the Unimaginable at breakneck speed to reach his longed-for destination.

At last, he would find the mountain and claim Old's gold.

Number Seven of the First Ones could taste the air of freedom as jubilation hugged his senses.

And then, inexplicably, the void stopped, slamming Neves On into its unyielding, dark walls.

'Move!' Neves On wailed, but nothing happened. Alarm gripped his throat as surely as the mottle-coated wolf had gripped Benny's that morning.

'Why have we stopped?' Neves On battered the walls of his dark capsule with one hand, whilst the other gripped the unicorn wand, white-knuckled.

'Why are we still?' he screeched in disbelief.

The walls of the void barely let him move and with terrifying brilliance, the visions resurged.

The little unicorn stood fully grown.

Distraught, Neves On watched the herd disappear from sight. He howled like a captive animal.

Too soon, the Ritual of Return was mended!

'Let me out!' But the dark fluid walls held him, barely acknowledging the sound. Something as basic as a sob clutched his throat. 'Let me go!' he wheezed, and there was no echo. He could not sit or move. Standing in his restricted tunnel, he swayed within its liquid walls.

Fury tore at his chest. He gripped the Staff of the Unimaginable unthinkingly hard then almost dropped her in amazement.

For only the fourth time since he had robbed her from her true calling, the white wand spoke, but this time, she sang. In a voice made golden, she fluted stoically in their captive tunnel.

I ask a question
This I ask of you
Is doing right
Even if your heart should break
A greater thing than being happy
Whichever means that might take?

I ask a question
This I ask of you
Does a cheerful coward
Have greater worth
Than a hero
Who is sad but true?

I ask a question
This I ask of you
How are we judged
At the last
Is it by the length of life
Or what we do from end to start?

I ask a question
This I ask of you
In times of need
When all seems lost
Whom do we call to help our cause
Whom do we beg at any cost?

I ask a question
This I ask of you

Is power borrowed
Yours to keep
Or will it leave
And let you weep?

The Staff of the Unimaginable stopped her song as swiftly as she had begun.

Spellbound by the charm of her voice, the sorcerer held her uncertainly. Moments passed, revealing the helplessness of his situation. He was trapped in a corridor of his own vision, his own making, as the white wand sang taunting words.

So, it seemed his luck had run out, mere seconds before he achieved freedom.

A snarl curled his lip. 'You mock me,' he whispered to the wand and the walls. 'You mock me unfairly.'

The Staff of the Unimaginable trebled a single note in response, as her centre lit, in a blaze of white light.

The sorcerer grinned. She would still do his bidding. She would light his way and somehow make it possible for him to reach his goal. As if reading his mind, her white light faded and all that was left was a dull, red glow.

'Get me out of here,' Number Seven of the First Ones, growled. 'Set me free from this infernal trap. Do my bidding now, pretty one, or you will never see a unicorn again.'

CHAPTER 17

Slither hither thither

Bibs heard the eagle call one more time, but the sound was so distant that it could hardly be heard. Dumbfounded by his surroundings and his great good luck, Bibs slid slowly on. Looking up then left to right, he felt smaller and less significant than he had ever felt in his life.

'Old's gold,' he muttered, 'Old's gold. These must be Old's caves.'

He stopped and listened. Not even the forest had been so silent. He could hear something, but he wasn't sure what it was. It boomed and thudded in a constant rhythm. He decided to keep moving. Hopefully he could get far away from whatever the thudding was.

Bibs moved on, passing through a portal that took him to another cave. In its centre there flowed a small waterfall that coursed smoothly through an opening in the mountain, before it streamed away into dim recesses.

Vast golden patches of wall lit the cave with a muted glow, lighting the way. He slid to the centre of the grotto. There was writing etched into a patch of floor in enormous swirling letters!

As surely as if Old were present, Bibs could sense the First One. He looked up, certain he would see him, but of course, Old wasn't there.

Bibs slumped sadly. He had a memory of Old smiling broadly from his half-moon mouth as he strode resolutely along in his plain brown robe. How wonderful if Old had been there to show the unicorns, and his brothers, his caves! Trying hard not to be despondent, Bibs read the words etched into the floor.

Like a candle in the wind
The petal draws strength from its core

Bibs sat back and held his breath. The booming sound had gone, to be replaced by the trickle of the waterfall. Breathing normally, he read the words again. How like Old to write something like that. Bibs grinned. Old had been full of quiet wisdom, and sometimes, not so quiet! His heart ached. Old had been special. Why did he have to leave them all? Immediately, Bibs was reminded of the Sorcerer of Great Contempt. It was the sorcerer's fault that Old was gone!

Bibs cast a look over his shoulder. So far, the caves seemed empty of any other life. Afraid of the vast loneliness of the place, he slid quickly away, glancing over his shoulder as he went.

Old's caves had many, many chambers. For all Bibs knew, the sorcerer or one of his tame creatures might be hiding there. Perhaps that was the eagle's plan.

Bibs gulped. Perhaps he, Bibs, was being used to lure the sorcerer or his creatures from a place of hiding. He thought of the words etched into the floor. *Like a candle in the wind, the petal draws strength from its core*. Bibs took heart from them. He must now be strong, not silly. If the eagle had wanted him dead he would have eaten him, and as for using him as bait, how absurd! Even as Bibs had the thought, the booming sound began.

Trying to escape the noise, Bibs slid fearfully into a new cave. It was tiny compared to the vast chambers of mountain rooms that he had just gone through, but this one was made entirely of gold. It was very bright. Not a piece of wall or floor remained made of dirt or stone.

Something caught his eye on the farthest wall. He couldn't see it well, but there was something there. Nervously, he moved to take a closer look. As he did so, the booming grew louder.

It was a doorknob! It was bright blue and the only thing in the entire chamber that wasn't made of gold. Bibs sighed in disgust. Snails, even Imperial Guards, could not open door knobs! They were forced to leave that kind of thing to others. Bibs wondered what he should do. What was beyond that door? Maybe there were things best left unseen. After all, he was a snail on his own. It was obvious he could not enter, so there was no point in fretting over what couldn't be done.

The silence deepened and the distant booming threatened to overwhelm him. Bibs peered uncertainly around. He didn't want to be a coward; he wanted to make Old proud. He thought of the message written in the floor and realised it gave him something to hold on to.

'Like a candle in the wind, the petal draws strength from its core,' he whispered, as he tried to comfort himself. As soon as he stopped speaking, he heard creaking.

'What was that?' he breathed. A cold shiver crawled along his skin. He didn't dare look around. Almost in a plea to Old's spirit, he shut his eyes.

'Like a candle in the wind, the petal draws strength from its core,' he stated boldly. Perhaps, if he said it long, loud and hard enough, he too would draw strength. The creaking grew louder.

'Like a candle in the wind, the petal draws strength from its core!' Bibs shouted the words as he braced himself for the worst, still hoping Old would be proud of him, in some odd way.

The creaking groaned throughout the chamber and then, with a loud bang, a blast of air brushed warmly past him.

Bibs waited. The booming surged.

Bibs couldn't bear it; he just had to know. Turning quickly, he faced where the blast of warm air had come from. He gasped. The patch of golden wall with the bright blue doorknob had opened, in a kind of rough-hewn entrance!

But how?

Bibs turned and peered into the opening. More gold greeted his eyes. He had an idea.

'Like a candle in the wind,' he said, and then watched closely.

The rough-hewn door began to quiver.

'The petal,' he paused, as the door inched around, 'draws strength from its core!' he finished with a bellow.

The door pushed wide open. Bibs grinned in triumph. At last he had done something right! Accidentally, he was willing to admit, but he had done it!

'The verse,' he giggled, 'it was the verse!'

Without waiting another moment, he slid quickly through the chamber, and just as he was passing the door, a new idea came to him. He stopped, paused, and waited several moments. The silence deepened and the booming beat on.

Bibs grinned cunningly, and then coughed. The booming went away for a moment but then returned. He danced a little jig. Once again the booming stopped when Bibs made a noise. He stood still, waiting for the booming to return. He grinned openly and giggled out loud then chortled furiously. Soon, he was laughing so hard that tears of glee poured down his face. Finally, controlling himself, he looked ahead. The secret chamber beckoned. As the stillness descended once more, the booming rhythm returned.

Bibs grinned. 'Be still my beating heart,' he said out loud to no one but himself.

CHAPTER 18

The dark of the storm
Shall whisper your name

Will trembled and rocked on his heels, not daring to open his eyes. The hard rock of the mountain pressed unyieldingly into his back, even as the Wand of Time suffused warmth into his hands. Keeping his eyes closed, Will pressed a hand against the mountain wall and felt around as far as he could. Sheer and cold, the mountain gave nothing to hope for. He took several deep breaths but they caught in his throat. The thought of looking down made him ill, so he continued to press as far back with his body as he could. His thumb nervously twitched into the wand, making her hum, and then sing.

The dark of the storm
Shall whisper your name

Adventure and venture
Are only for the game

Let go of attachment
And all will be revealed

*Let yourself leap
And your fear you will heal.*

Will was in no mood for taking leaps of any kind.

'Stop it,' he growled from between clenched teeth, 'stop it! I'm not brave! I'm not attached to anything! I'm jammed here and heaven help us if there is a storm, let alone it whispering my name, or whatever it is you're going on about!'

The Wand of Time struck a high note that made Will gasp and cover his ears. Immediately, he regretted the move. Swaying, his left foot slipped as rocks beneath him crumbled, and his right foot slithered. In a fragile effort of futility, he steadied himself and opened his eyes. Looking down, he almost laughed, despite his terror.

A shadow crossed the sun. Glancing up, he saw the eagle was once more hovering, once more pinning him with warm auburn eyes.

'Help me,' he cried out to the bird, 'help!'

Despite the sky's placid indifference, his call bounced off the solid rock-face, echoing for the world to hear.

In a lightning-fast move, the eagle boldly screeched in his face. Gasping, Will looked down again.

Like an impossible apparition, a winding gift of stairs was carved into the mountain, directly beneath him. *So, he hadn't imagined it!* He glanced sideways. The eagle coasted placidly beside him.

'Why,' Will wheezed, 'would there be a staircase carved on the outside of a mountain? Who would do such a thing?'

Peering down, he could not see where the stairs ended, no matter how hard he tried. He barely had time to wonder what it meant when the eagle brushed him with an outstretched wing. Will flinched and, in doing so, noticed that despite the day's beauty, a storm gathered menacingly in the distance. Small flickers of chill wind gusted thickly from the darkening sky. Will understood that there was no time to lose.

Sick to his stomach, he clutched the Wand of Time and took his first step. The staircase was real! He exhaled raggedly, still terrified but relieved. Despite the plunge that confronted him should he slip, he knew a bright flicker of hope.

Thunder groaned in the distance.

The eagle soared by Will's side, but then it veered, calling shrilly, and flew away. Will felt lost without it and hoped it would return.

In short, sharp bursts, squalls began to buffet him. Desperate, Will balanced on the walking wand. Steadfastly, she helped him to stay on his feet. From time to time, the wand glowed at her centre, as if showing him her light would give him strength. Formidably, the storm gathered, slashing bolts of lightning to the innocent earth.

The stairs continued to unwind beneath Will in what seemed a never-ending downward spiral. He began to tire. Breathing in sharp gasps, he watched his footing, exhaustively. It was tricky descending steps that were worn by rain, sun and all kinds of weather, until they had become almost as slippery as glass. Several times, if not for the walking wand, Will might have plunged to the valley below.

The winds became insistent. Wilder gusts flung harshly at Will, forcing him to lean on the Wand of Time, again and again. With no idea where the steps ended, Will knew one thing: he must not be on the stairs when the storm arrived. As he had the thought, the sun disappeared. He stopped to catch his breath, and looked up.

Like a malevolent wraith, the storm had crept forward. Will choked back dread as he and the storm faced one another. With brooding abandon, dense, muddy clouds churned and spun around him. Then the clouds hugged Will, and his world went dark. Into the gloom, the Wand of Time blazed from her centre in an effort to illuminate the way. Moisture from the clouds made the steps impossibly greasy. Will collapsed onto his knees as freezing air lashed him.

'It's not going to happen,' he sobbed, 'it's never going to happen.'

Hot tears froze to Will's cheeks. He pulled the wand toward his chest where she blazed keenly for him, trying to send him warmth. Will felt his knees freeze to the rock. Dazed and defeated, he held the wand close. Once again that day, the Wand of Time struck a high note that shocked him from his stupor.

Almost dropping her from the force of her cry, Will fell to his hands, his knuckles grinding painfully into rock.

The storm growled around him. It was a warning.

The wand beamed her light as brightly as she could. Amazed, Will found he could see the step he was kneeling on. New hope glimmered timidly within him. Crawling, he lowered himself to the step below. Taking heart, he crawled downward again, slipping only a little. He made the next step as well.

The storm groaned, then crackled and roared.

The knuckles of Will's hand that clutched the wand were soon shredded and bleeding, but he crept on. His knees, too, were raw where his trousers had torn, but he was making progress. In the thick of the clouds, his teeth chattered and his body shook so hard that moving, despite the pain it brought him, was an agonising blessing.

Surely he would reach the end soon.

And then the storm struck with a snarl that flogged Will to his core. Thunder and lightning defied everything in its path as the storm challenged the mountain with currents of power, illuminating the valley below, for eerie, flickering seconds.

Will wondered if the lightning would catch him and cook him like a bug. He needed to cover his ears, but he knew that was impossible. He continued crawling and slithering as well as he knew how, his elbows skinned and cut to the bone from dropping downwards on to each new step. Vowing he would reach his destination, whatever it was, or die trying, he fell into a daze of waking unreality.

Deafened by the roar of angry currents, Will wondered if he had ever done anything other than crawl down these slippery, treacherous steps. In fact he could not think of, or remember, another time and place. *Perhaps his whole life could be summed up by the task at hand.* His mind was exhausted and his body was beyond his command. It almost made greater sense to lie down and sleep.

Just as he had the thought, Will slammed head-first into something hard. He lay, stunned, while the storm romped, deranged, around him. Warmth flooded Will's bones. He no longer felt the pain of his battered body. He smiled secretly to himself. This wasn't so bad; in fact, it was really quite pleasant. The fingers that gripped the walking wand unclamped their hold. Will breathed deeply as his eyes closed.

The storm revelled, sending small rocks of ice into the world. Lightning struck and lit the atmosphere with broken shards of dancing radiance.

Barely conscious, Will was beginning to feel at home.

'I dreamed I had a magic wand,' he sighed, 'and she was so very beautiful.'

In his half-open hand, the Wand of Time glowed.

Before them there were no more steps. Instead, a door made of time-worn wood nestled into the mountain rock-face. That is what Will had hit with his head.

As if in answer to another touch, the Wand of Time stirred. The walking wands were made to answer their masters, but these were strange times. The Wand of Time began to sing.

I dream of home
I dream of a place
Where I have been

I am now home
I am now home
I am brought to my master's lair

Awaken young man
Awake young Will
Open the prize and all will be known.

It is doubtful Will ever understood what woke him. Without having consciously heard the wand's song, he rose. As if he had been doing it every day of his life, he planted his feet squarely against the buffeting storm and placed a hand on the great brass knob to the old wooden door.

'There you are,' he whispered, with chattering, clamped lips. 'There you are, at last.'

With all the strength left to him, Will turned the handle, stepped through the opening, and walked inside the mountain. The door slammed shut behind him, cutting the hail, sleet and madness completely away.

Warm air flooded Will's senses. He held the Wand of Time against his cheek and took several deep breaths.

'We're home,' he whispered. And in a moment of complete release, he collapsed, fainting onto the safety of the cave's floor.

The Wand of Time fell from his hand then and lay quietly, waiting for her young master to awake.

CHAPTER 19

Purple patch... purple patch... purple patch

Flightlord and Far glanced meaningfully at each other. At last, everything was silent and nothing rattled the sixteenth door. They sighed with relief.

In Hope's room, the pots of boiling moat mud on the window sills, bubbled as furiously as ever. A splash of purple medicine that had missed Flightlord's mouth stained the floor in garish colour.

Cross-eyed from watching the butterfly sit on his nose, Flightlord managed to keep his dignity.

'How are you feeling?' Far whispered, peering at Flightlord with cautious concern. She leaned forward and examined his face carefully for signs of change.

'I'm not sure,' Flightlord grunted.

'Has *anything* changed?' Far grumbled. The dragon looked no different. Disappointed, she sat back with a despondent scowl.

Flightlord moved his tail and then he moved his legs.

'Maybe,' he murmured.

Impatiently, Far left his nose and flew to look at the wound on his side. She fluttered in the air, making choking sounds.

'Get up!' she finally bellowed.

Surprised, Flightlord sat up.

'Get *up*,' Far growled. 'I mean, get up off the floor and stand!'

The dragon took orders from no one. In another time and place, her manner and tone might have been the end of her, but the bright blue butterfly was his cherished friend. Ignoring her rudeness, Flightlord stood.

Far pointed to his side. 'Turn around and look at your behind!' she squealed.

Flightlord filled Hope's room, so turning to do anything in the limited space was almost impossible. As much as he tried, he found that his movements were blocked. One thing was for sure: he was no longer in pain. He tried to wiggle his body, but books fell from tables, and potions rattled on shelves.

He looked at Far. 'I think I'd best go outside,' he murmured.

'You can't!' Far snapped.

Flightlord raised an eyebrow. She was his friend, but he would only take so much of being ordered around.

Far flew to the other side of the room, suspecting she had pushed her luck. Settling on some books, she explained in an appeasing tone.

'I am reluctant to open the common door, in case something tries to enter.'

Flightlord nodded as he moved an enormous foot and brought a hand up to scratch his nose, but even as he did so, he bumped some shelves and sent a small bottle of something interesting-looking, rolling around.

Far frowned. He was right. He was much too big to stay inside.

She fluttered cautiously to the peep-hole of the common door, and looked out. All seemed clear so she quickly flew to the windows and looked outside. The sky still brooded, but the dark green corruption of whatever had erupted in Wish was breaking up. Glimpses of blue peeped from the unfortunate sky.

Far turned to Flightlord. 'Alright,' she agreed, 'I'll open the common door, but you must run out as fast you can. Is it a deal?'

Flightlord nodded cheerfully. 'Thanks for all your help,' he smiled, 'whatever was in that bottle of purple stuff, it seems to have fixed my trouble.'

Far simply nodded. Pronouncing the secret word under her breath, the common door flung open.

Knocking over a small table and a basket of scrolls, Flightlord rushed through the door, which immediately slammed behind him. He stood in the hall of the tower, marvelling at how well he felt. Just a short time ago, he had been painfully wounded and barely able to breathe. He wriggled his hands and feet; they were fine. Deciding that it should be safe, he went outside. He slit his eyes to pin-pricks and scanned the landscape. Large patches of blue sky showed, as remnants of angry clouds scudded away. Satisfied that all seemed normal, Flightlord remembered Far's request.

Mystified, he twisted around to look at his behind. He gasped. But this was a disaster! His whole side was *purple*. The wound was gone, and he was grateful for that, but his bottom and side were purple!

Flightlord growled, mortified with shame. He tried to hide the stain with one hand but that didn't work. He put both hands on his side to cover it up, then tried to walk but that didn't work either. He peered around. No one was watching, and that was just as well. He had his dignity to consider! Rainbow dragons, despite the name, did not get about in any colour other than a nice, plain green. He grimaced; he would be laughed at. Dragons did not take well to being laughed at!

He dashed to the moat and jumped in, spreading sticky black moat mud over his bottom. The moat mud slid straight off. He lay down in the moat and did his best to scrub the purple away. Putting his head under water, he tried to peer between his legs to see if his back end was clean. Water rushed up his nostrils and he snorted upward for air.

Was anyone watching? Was anyone laughing?

With a mighty leap, he flung himself from the moat to land near Hope's windows. He turned to look at his bottom. It was still purple. Perhaps it was temporary? Frowning fearsomely, he turned to Hope's room.

A little face was pressed against the window pane with a worried look.

Flightlord's heart melted. How could he be angry with the butterfly, when she had probably saved his life? Nonetheless, he stormed up to her.

Bravely, Far faced Flightlord. Now she might lose her friend.

Powering up to the window, Flightlord stopped and glared.

Far gazed back at him with huge molten eyes that begged his forgiveness.

The dragon had tremendous pride in his appearance, as did all rainbow dragons. What would he tell the other dragons? That he had been wounded? A thing unheard of in dragon circles! How could he explain that he had received healing from a *butterfly?* Or that he had accepted an untried potion and had become half purple? It didn't bear thinking about. His head rocked. He would be scorned!

Sadly, Far peered up at Flightlord's angry face. *This is it then,* she thought. *There will be no one to talk to until the day Hope returns... if he ever does.* It was a lonely prospect. She took her face away from the window and turned to fly away.

'Stop right there,' Flightlord boomed.

Far knew he wouldn't hurt her, but she turned, resigned, knowing that now he would yell and she would feel bad.

'Because of you,' he began, 'I look foolish!'

Far nodded and said nothing.

Flightlord puffed himself up and twisted around to look at his rear. Turning back to Far, he glared.

'Because of you, I will now be laughed at by every dragon and creature I meet!'

Far nodded again and slumped sadly onto the window ledge. It had been a terrible day. She waited for the next thing he would say, with her head bowed, but nothing happened and finally, she looked up.

Flightlord was still there, but he was grinning from ear to ear.

What was this?

'And because of you,' he boomed, 'I have no pain, my wound is healed and I am alive and well!'

Far sat up. 'But what about the other dragons and all the creatures who will laugh at you?' she called through the window.

'Let them laugh!' Flightlord roared, as if challenging the world. 'Let everyone laugh if they want to! I could care less what they think. After all, how many dragons do you know that are half-purple?'

Far giggled and Flightlord grinned.

Together they began to chuckle. Just as the last black-green cloud disappeared from the sky, they were laughing so hard that it was easy to believe that the morning had never been ugly or dangerous in any way.

On the floor in Hope's room, the now empty bottle of purple potion lay. Written on the label was the inscription: For creatures of cold blood.

However, in the fine print that Far had been too rushed to notice, there was other writing:

Side effects: Possible dizzy spells and purple patches. Recommended dosage: Only 2 drops for all creatures and no more!

CHAPTER 20

On the horns of a dilemma

Taken aback by the shock of power that coursed through her, Rielle held the Wand of Faith at arm's length. Hope went to claim his wand immediately, but something stopped him. Instead, he stepped aside with a measured tread, and watched Rielle attentively.

The wand beamed brightly from her centre light and hummed softly in a gentle murmur. The herd and First Ones looked on, amazed. How could this be? The walking wands sang only for those who wielded them!

As Rielle gaped, stunned, the wand began to sing.

In days gone by
Don't ask me why
Time stood still
Or drifted until
Things became a certain way
Shifting slowly day by day

But now things move and change we know
Never the same

Time to grow
Expect to see the shape of things
Turn to other
Other whims

The voice that whispers
In thick and thin
Reveals itself to the listener within
A hunch, a feeling, an omen or such
Is the warning
Of very much

Ask who holds me in this hour
Ask who holds and knows my power
Ask if she is more than before
Ask why I sing
And then ask why
I am not mute or a stranger to her.

The Wand of Faith stopped singing and her centre light went out. Only the whisper of keening winds rustled on the mountainside.

Rielle turned to Hope. Wordless and dumbfounded, she handed back his wand. Passing a hand over her face, she brushed unexplained tears from her cheeks. She was tired and overwhelmed. Will was gone, and now this peculiar occurrence with the wand. She glanced at the herd. They studied her intently.

'What?' Rielle whispered. 'What is it? Why are you all watching me like that?' No one answered and nothing moved.

It was Hope who placed a comforting hand on her shoulder.

'These are strange times,' he murmured. 'Don't let it worry you, young Rielle.' He smiled down at her and then, thoughtfully, strode away. With his back turned to everyone, he stood quietly for a while, at some distance.

Rielle was edgy. Why had the wand sung for her and beamed its centre light? She knew it wasn't supposed to. Wands only spoke or glowed for those who were honoured to wield them. What exactly had happened? She tore her eyes from Hope's back and looked at the herd. She met a wall of velvet eyes.

'I don't understand what happened,' Rielle whispered, looking directly at Candela. 'Why did the wand sing for me?'

Candela's knowing eyes glowed. 'You have done nothing wrong my dear,' she murmured readily. 'We are all... well... perhaps startled, but maybe not completely surprised.'

Hope turned. His face was shadowed with unreadable thoughts.

'There has been no harm done, Rielle,' he assured. 'We have many more pressing matters to worry about right now.'

Rielle hung her head. 'I'm sorry,' she murmured, 'I know we have to think about what happened to Will, and Bibs.' Her breath shuddered on the words.

Pud leaned into her and nudged her hand.

Oobaat cleared his throat. 'It looks badly.' He gestured toward the cliff. 'If what we see here is correctly deduced, then....' He paused and raised an eyebrow. He stroked his chin. 'However, to deduce can sometimes be a premature thing.' He held up a hand as Rielle frowned at him.

'Wait,' he pressed, almost urgently. 'Perhaps this is not quite what it seems.' He turned and looked at the broken cliff. 'But, if it is, remember my friends, that Will *does* wield the Wand of Time. That is not insignificant.'

'Yes,' Coraggio murmured, 'we must not jump to final conclusions.'

Little Bobs called out. 'What about all these footprints that the rain didn't wash away? What about the hat? It's a long way to fall down,' he exclaimed. 'I can't see anything other than… than… you know, rocks and stuff, and way down there, the valley. That's all!'

Surprised, they all turned to see little Bobs peering over the cliff edge.

'Get away from there,' Oobaat stressed urgently, but not unkindly. 'We can't risk you falling, our good, young friend!'

Little Bobs didn't budge. 'Bibs *was* with him, wasn't he?' Bibs glared as if hoping to be told otherwise, yet it was obvious that no matter what anyone said, he would not believe them.

In that moment, Rielle unhappily understood how much the young snail had changed; how much less trusting he had become.

'We don't know that,' Coraggio exclaimed, 'but if you don't get away from there yourself, you might be next!'

Little Bobs blushed, mortified to be scolded by a unicorn. He slid to Oobaat and looked up at him, as if Oobaat had the answers.

With a quiet nod of his head, Oobaat hunkered down.

'Have courage, little Bobs,' he murmured kindly. 'At this stage we can be sure of nothing. We must simply take each situation as it comes.'

Round-eyed, little Bobs nodded.

Oobaat stood and faced the gathering. 'We are in the most unenviable position ever,' he began. 'We have become separated from some of our group and that is very bad.'

The herd shifted.

'What we do now is what counts.' Coraggio stepped into the conversation. 'We have decisions to make.' He looked meaningfully around. 'Do we hunt for our friends? Or do we continue to search for Old's caves?'

Oobaat and Hope nodded, as the herd shifted uneasily. Hope shook his head slowly and thoughtfully. Oobaat stepped forward to speak and the strength of his feelings was such that the Staff of Life briefly hummed.

'A moral dilemma,' he whispered, 'a moral dilemma is just what Neves On, no doubt, would want for us right now!'

'No doubt,' Coraggio agreed, 'no doubt. But do we let this stop us? No, of course we can't.'

Hope paced up and down. 'The one thing we must assume,' he stated, 'is that our brother, Number Seven, is free.' He looked at Oobaat, who nodded in agreement. 'So,' Hope continued, 'perhaps, and this is not set in stone, but perhaps, although we have an obligation to Will and Bibs, is it not vitally important to secure and safeguard the gold in Old's caves? In case, well, in case

Neves On reaches it first, then finds the secret to eternal life. He will wreak havoc with that kind of power!'

Coraggio nodded. 'So what you are saying,' he breathed, 'is that despite the fact that we owe it to be there for our dear friends, whom, for all we know, are completely defenceless, ultimately, well ultimately, we must hope beyond all hope that they are, at best, able to cope for now. At worst, well, they may already be laid to rest.' He looked at everyone there, as if testing the weight of his next words. 'In other circumstances, we would split up; some of us would go to seek our friends and some would continue on our mission. However, if we split now, we risk losing much-needed strength. No, that is just what Number Seven would want. We owe it to all that is good and true, to secure Old's gold and keep it from falling into the wrong hands.' He finished the last sentence fervently.

'Yes,' Oobaat reluctantly agreed. 'Despite the fact it may look heartless, if we have the power to keep all worlds safe from unlimited evil, well, then we must think carefully what to do.' Looking pensive and uncomfortable, he whispered the next words with his eyes flaming. 'The greater good lies in the balance.'

No one spoke as the situation became clearer. Winds stopped rustling. Even the mountain seemed to pause. Overhead, the timeless call of an eagle prompted Candela to step forward. She gazed kindly from knowing eyes.

'It is important that we weigh each prospect, otherwise we may never know the importance of making a choice... a decision. We must, as with all things, despite the pain it often brings us, we *must* decide, and then press on.'

Coraggio stepped forward. 'We need to make our decision clearly, and without regret… now.'

Rielle felt tears rise in her throat. She looked at the broken cliff and wished with all her heart that she could bring Will and Bibs back. She walked to where Hope had placed Will's hat on the ground. Tenderly, she picked it up. She turned to the others.

'I'll take care of this,' she breathed.

Without another word, Coraggio, Candela and the unicorn herd turned from the cliff edge and looked toward the mountain. With quiet yet speedy steps, the herd led the way to search for Old's caves. The decision had been made. The others followed.

Rielle didn't move immediately. She turned Will's hat in her hands.

'If you're out there, Will and Bibs,' she whispered, so quietly that only Pud heard, 'then I promise that once we're done with protecting Old's gold, I won't rest until I know what has happened to you both.'

Walking ahead, Hope turned and looked kindly at her.

'Come, young Rielle,' he called, 'a girl who can wield a wand made for First Ones must not be left behind.'

Rielle turned and looked once more at the broken cliff. A furrow crossed her brow. A large black bird sat at the edge of the cliff and watched her quietly, with yellow eyes.

Rielle glanced to see if Hope had seen it, but Hope was beckoning her with a smile. She shook her head. *Perhaps grief was making her see things that weren't there.*

Pud pushed eagerly against her. Turning away, Rielle

ran with him to catch up to the group.

Hope smiled comfortingly down at her. 'Remember,' he murmured, 'that things may not always be as they seem.'

As if the mountain knew that something vital had happened, it rumbled, threw rocks at them, groaned and spat, then settled to let them go on.

Rielle looked once more to the cliff, but the black bird was gone.

CHAPTER 21

Catch me if you dare

The Sorcerer of Great Contempt squinted with livid eyes at the Staff of the Unimaginable. The wand stood starkly white against the black walls of the sorcerer's self-made tunnel.

'Get me out of here,' Neves On urged, 'set me free from this infernal trap. I promise,' he hissed through gritted teeth, 'that if you show me how to escape then I will let you see unicorns again.'

The wand shifted slightly against the wall and, in so doing, rolled and fell with a thud against him. The hard bump of the wood grazed the newly healed wound on his leg. He grimaced and cursed.

'You test me, white wood,' he snarled, 'you test my patience in many ways.' Carefully, he returned her to the dark wall.

The unicorn wand glowed red.

'Time runs out as I stand here waiting,' Neves On spat.

A muscle in his cheek twitched. He tried to cast his mind to the unicorn herd and the First Ones, but now his visions were blocked. He strove harder to see where they were and what they were doing, but he could see nothing.

'Protection,' he slammed, 'they have increased their protection. Everything has protection!'

With a curse, he punched the wall of his captivity but it merely shifted jelly-like at the impact, with a dull thud. Neves On began to laugh. Arms akimbo, he turned in his small tunnel until laughter filled it.

'Foiled, but not for long,' he mocked, wiping tears of amusement from his eyes.

How to proceed?

He picked up the wand and turned her in both hands. One of her ends scraped the side of a dark wall and she uttered a shrill note, as if in protest. Neves On placed her gently down then turned his back on her.

Unexpectedly, the dark capsule shook and twirled wildly, throwing the sorcerer into its walls. With nothing to hold on to, Neves On was tossed and buffeted until he could barely stand. Once again, to his shame and horror, panic rose in his chest.

'What is it?' he cried. 'What's happening now?'

As if in answer to his call, the Staff of the Unimaginable twanged so shrilly that he had to cover his ears. Barely able to stand still long enough to see, he did his best to look at her. The wand wasn't moving.

'How can you be so still?' he bellowed.

In a short pause that let him catch his breath, he peered closely at her. Where one of her tips touched the dark mass of wall, the unicorn wand was streaming white light, and the light was making a hole.

'What are you doing?' he raged. 'If you break this capsule, who knows where we'll end up or what could happen to us?'

The Staff of the Unimaginable ignored him, seeming to push harder into the wall's fabric. The hole was growing quickly. Like a punctured balloon, the capsule began to bucket and roll.

The sorcerer called again for the wand to stop, but it was too late. One entire dark wall evaporated, sending a rush and groan of hot air to envelop him. He lunged for the wand, just as she was about to disappear into the unknown.

'You aren't getting rid of me that easily,' he wheezed.

His hand barely managed to close over her before he, too, began to fall. Touching her scores constantly, he winced, agonised by her merciless burns. The emptiness they fell through was dank and dark. Hot air blasted them ruthlessly.

Eerily, of her own accord, the Staff of the Unimaginable chanted:

Are we captive?
Are we caught?
Are we lost?
Or are we naught?

Do we count?
Do we matter?
Do we land?
Or do we splatter?

Is this real?
Is this not?
Is this justice?
Or a plot?

Will this dark never end?
Will this place be our home?
Will this gloom go on forever?
Is there a landing in this tomb?

What say YOU Neves On?
What will you DO Neves On?
What will BE Neves On?
Do something NOW Neves On!

'You're supposed to help me!' bellowed the sorcerer, as the speed of their fall engulfed him. In response, the wand twanged and bit him so hard that he almost dropped her.

'You... you!' he began to threaten but quickly checked himself. She might be challenging him at every step, but he needed her power. Pure hatred for the unicorn wand flooded through him, but he checked that too. No matter how he felt about her, she was the bearer of ultimate power. What had she just chanted to him? *Do something?* So, she was not going to help him. Then he had better do something indeed! Despite the dizziness that clutched him, he gritted his teeth and put his mind to work.

What did he want? He wanted the outside world!

With a grimace, he realised that he was becoming lazy

and dependent on the wand; that he was neglecting to use his own powers. *He must not allow that to happen.* Hot air swept past, threatening to suffocate him. *He must think quickly.* There was only one place he wanted to be and he wanted that so powerfully that his bones and jaw ached.

'To the outside world! Take me to the outside world!' he croaked into the hot air of the emptiness.

At first, nothing happened.

Just as Number Seven of the First Ones began to wonder if he had indeed lost his touch, the darkness lifted. He sucked his teeth and held his breath. A leer crossed his face. A rush of steaming air pounded the sorcerer, as he and the Staff of the Unimaginable landed with terrific force into salty water.

Plunging with the power of the crash, Neves On clung to the white wand, dragging her through the depths with him. In his mind, he grinned.

He was in the outside world! Surely the mountain could not be far?

The wand felt extremely heavy, as if water made her turn to lead. With only one hand free, the Sorcerer of Great Contempt pushed upward to the surface. Gasping for air, he gave a great shout of elation. Holding the wand, he saluted with both arms to the ethers.

He was free! Free of Wish! Free of restraint! Free!

CHAPTER 22

Keep the gold for time

Bibs slid into the secret chamber. The rough-hewn door closed behind him with a sharp snap. Surprised, he noted that on this side, there was not so much as a handle; the door had become part of the wall. Slightly worried but also mesmerised, he slid slowly around, looking left and right. To call it a cave would have been unfair.

This had to be where Old had made his home. It had to be!

Being a snail, Bibs knew little of others' homes, but he had been to the Tower of Dreams, and to Hope's room. This was similar except for one major thing: everything here was made of gold. The round table in the middle of the room was gold, as were the chairs, the cupboards, the plates and spoons, the things that sat idly on the benches and also the walls: all gold. Even a golden blanket was folded neatly at the end of the small cot bed. It was a cheery little room, and again, Bibs felt as if Old were there.

'Are you here?' he whispered, looking around. 'Are you here, Eerht ytnewt On?' Bibs waited but then felt silly. Of course Old was not there!

'Old's gold eh?' he muttered. 'But what does it all mean?'

Bibs reflected on his current situation. Was it just luck that he was there? Had the eagle placed him there by accident or was this some kind of plan? After all, what good did it do for him to be there while the others were still searching to find Old's caves?

Thoughts buzzed in his mind, confusing him. Nothing about this made any sense. He paused in his tracks. If nothing made any sense then could Will be alright? If nothing made any sense, then maybe, there was some kind of sense even in that.

He stopped in a small rut in the floor. He looked down. It wasn't a rut. It was more carved writing, but this time etched in gold. He read: *The Formula.*

Bibs' heart boomed. 'The Formula,' he whispered. 'The formula for what?'

He slid along the etching and continued reading: *Present... In the moment we are offered a gift.*

Annoyed, and wishing the others were there, Bibs slid as fast as he could around the message, reading it again and again until he made himself dizzy. Was that all it was meant to say? Frustrated at feeling so useless and unable to do anything, he called aloud to the golden walls.

'What formula? What present? What gift? What? What? What does it mean?' Nothing moved inside the chamber.

Bibs slid to the fireplace of the golden den and, from sheer annoyance, he blew onto the large pile of unused coals sitting in the grate. Like an eruption, the coals burst into flame, almost singeing poor Bibs and scaring him so thoroughly that he raced to the other side of the room.

Turning to the wall where the door had been, he called out in panic. 'Like a candle in the wind, the petal draws strength from its core!' Nothing happened. The door that had let him in did not open to let him out.

Bibs looked back at the fire. The whole room vibrated, crackling with tremendous vigour and fiery life. Coils of smoke bellowed through a small chimney that had been built cleverly in the ceiling.

By some strange stroke of the fire's light, part of the etching on the floor had become brightly lit. Curiously, Bibs peered at the writing. In the shadow of the flames, certain letters stood out. *Sent omen*, they read. Bibs screwed up his nose. *Sent omen?* That made no sense at all. Obviously it was just an arrangement of the fire's light.

He turned from the words and wandered around the room, keeping a safe distance from the fire. A dish on the floor contained water. Bibs slid over to drink. He wasn't to know that it was the very bowl that Pud had drunk from when he and Rielle had been there, before their roaming had taken them with Old, to Wish. Some dried-up crumbs of cake spattered the floor. Bibs ate them. They reminded him of something, but he couldn't think what.

Bemused, he slid back to the centre of the room. The fire crackled loudly and the walls glowed brightly. Perplexed, Bibs had no idea what to do next.

...

The Sorcerer of Great Contempt trod water and roared with deliberate triumph. Freedom was indeed sweet, no matter about the watery landing! The mountain in the distance beckoned. Neves On squinted. A long, thin spiral of smoke poured richly from a spot on Old's mountain. Number Seven of the First Ones grinned. There was life on that mountain and he intended to find out where!

...

'Look!' Little Bobs surprised the others with his sudden outburst.

The herd, First Ones, Rielle and Pud looked to where he pointed.

Rielle gasped. 'Smoke! It's smoke!' She turned, grinning, to the herd. 'It must be Will! It has to be Will!'

Hope and Oobaat joined Candela and Coraggio to step forward and contemplate what they saw. With a joined thought, they reached out toward the place where the smoke spiralled richly into the sky.

Watching them, Rielle's hopes plunged. She walked quickly up to them.

'It's not Will, is it?' Rielle asked crestfallen, as she eyed the smoke. 'It's something else.'

Coraggio turned and his dark eyes reflected a knowing eagerness that set the herd on alert in seconds.

'It sends a message,' he breathed eagerly, 'and now we run! We run as fast as this mountain will let us! Come,' he cried, 'speed is the only way now!'

With those words, no longer caring for soundless stealth and without further question, the group turned to flee toward the smoke's message.

Already in the first stage of gallop, Benny nudged Rielle.

'Quickly,' he beckoned, 'it breaks the rules of unicorns, but jump on my back. We cannot risk letting you lag behind. You will never keep up with us now! Jump! Onto my back! Quickly, now!'

With a gasp at the urgency of the moment, and surprised that the rule of riding unicorns should be broken, Rielle grabbed a handful of Benny's mane. Instinctively, she leapt on his tall, broad back.

Almost unseating her, Benny bound into full gallop in blinding seconds. Pud ran easily beside the unicorn. Oobaat scooped little Bobs up and carried him; it was something he'd never done before.

Rielle quickly found her balance. Curious, she peered at the smoke curling in the distance. She squinted. It had shaped a word! Although pummelled by the speed of the gallop, she tried to make sense of the scatter of letters.

It read: *Enon*. Rielle frowned, wondering what it reminded her of. The wind whipped her eyes and made them water but she looked up once more. Eno On! It *had* to mean that, and, Eno On, well... that was Oobaat! Oobaat was Eno On, Number One of the First Ones!

Who would send such a message? Who was asking for Number One of the First Ones? Rielle's heart surged but, of course, it couldn't be Old. Who, then, knew how to write messages in smoke, from his mountain?

The mountain, itself, rolled and grunted but then, as if sensing the group's determination, it groaned and sat still.

...

In Number Twenty Three's golden room, Bibs sighed deeply and settled sadly to wait.

'Useless again,' he said aloud to Old's room, 'I am useless again, no matter what I do.'

CHAPTER 23

I remember tea for sadness

Will heard voices, whisperings in the air. Bold flashes of white called his name, but just as he reached out to them, a dark, shapeless mass blotted the white from view. The darkness laughed and pointed a scornful finger of doom, but the swirling mass of white poured back and sent the darkness away.

Everything became silent. Then, from a distance, footsteps made their way toward him, pattering almost cheerfully. They stopped. Something gently touched his brow and things were said, but Will could not make out the words. The footsteps pattered away, and Will drifted safely, in a neutral place.

Next, he saw Rielle standing on a bare, windswept hill. She seemed older, no longer a girl, but her smile was just the same. She called to him from behind a hood and held out a hand. Pud sat beside her, white-whiskered, and his amber eyes searched Will's with a gaze that was almost human.

Rielle beckoned and Will knew that he must hurry to catch up to her. Running so hard that he felt the sinews in his legs ache and burn, Will was almost on the hill, almost there, as Rielle kept smiling and holding out her hand.

. . .

When he opened his eyes, the first thing Will knew was that he was not holding the Wand of Time. He bolted upright. The wand rested at his feet, and in the effort he made to reach for her, he felt shooting pain stab through his entire body. He gasped and then began to cough, unable to stop for a long time. Tears of pain coursed down his cheeks.

He realised that his knees and elbows were worn raw to the bone and that he could barely move. He tried to stand, but his muscles were so cramped, and his skin so badly cracked and bruised, that he called out unwillingly, against the pain. *This made his time on the ledge with the eagle feel like a gentle pastime.*

Helpless, he sat still with no choice but to wait. He tried to clasp the wand tightly, but his fingers were also wounded and cut to the bone; some were swollen beyond recognition. He cradled the wand instead. Taking several deep breaths, the coughing resumed.

More wretched than he had ever been, and with sweat staining his brow, he attempted to stand once more. The half-formed scabs on his knees cracked open and bled. Grinding his teeth, Will forced himself to his feet. Dizziness slammed against him and nausea clamped his stomach. He shut his eyes, breathing deeply, and once more he began to cough. Finally, wheezing, he took a small step. Involuntary tears still trickled down his face.

Planting the Wand of Time into the dirt floor, he leaned against her, like an old man. The Wand of Time hummed as his hand slid clumsily against her honey wood.

Will tried to speak, but his lips, too, were raw, as thirst

147

raged torridly in his throat. He coughed a joyless laugh and took stock of his surroundings. *He must be standing inside the mountain!*

Behind him, there was a time-worn door. Obviously he had walked through that door, but he had no memory of it. He looked away. There was no reason he would ever go through that door again. *Who would build a staircase on the outside of a mountain?*

Listening carefully, Will tried to hear whether the storm still raged, then realised that if scabs had formed on his wounds, there was no way of knowing how long he had lain there. *Had days gone by?* Judging by how thirsty he was, it was possible. The thought of his ordeal made him tremble, and he quickly did his best to dismiss it.

He thought of his dream. *Footsteps had pattered up to him and something had touched his brow.* Leaning heavily on the walking wand, he slowly raised a stiff, painful arm to search his brow with the clenched fingers of one hand. He drew his hand away and looked at it, surprised. A small smudge of gold lay thickly on his chafed fingertips. He peered up, expecting to see that something had dropped onto him from above, but there was no gold on the roof of the cavern he stood in. *Had the footsteps been real? Was there someone here?*

He examined his surroundings. Everything was brown, but as his eyes became accustomed to the light, he was delighted to see that the browns were a myriad of wonderful shades. Some distance in front of him, a cleft in the rock, barely metres wide, showed that the small area where he stood had been carved carefully from the mountain's innards.

Intrigued, despite his pain and plight, he shuffled like a broken image of himself, to where the narrow opening beckoned. What should have taken minutes took him ten times longer, but straining and panting, he reached the gap. A laneway continued on from it.

Cautiously, dragging his unbending right leg, Will shuffled under the cleft and out to the other side. Soft, muted light showed him a marvellous world he would not have thought possible. As rough and bedraggled as the mountain was on the outside, it was equally beautiful on the inside.

Pouring along the walls of the passageway like inner rainbows, every shade of brown and muted pink flowed through the soil of the walls and floor. Will tried to smile but winced. His cracked, unmoving lips froze like a grimace.

Small sounds rustled around him as if this was where the mountain's true purpose lived. Another noise began to filter through. It was the sound of trickling water! It was distant, but Will knew he must find its source.

Gathering his energy, and leaning heavily on the walking wand, he followed the sound, marvelling at the warmth inside the mountain. No wonder Old had survived so well, and no wonder Old had loved this place.

The laneway tracked straight and level for some time, but then plummeted and rose with surprising twists and turns.

Will's heart grew dismal as despondency scratched his mind. *Where was the water?*

Surprisingly, despite the mess his body was in, once

he became accustomed to moving, it seemed to help a little. The bleeding from his cracked scabs had stopped and his joints embraced the soft, warm air.

A scuttling sound gave Will an excuse to stop. Two large, blue lizards peered at him from damask eyes, and then, as if it was something they did every day, they approached him instead of scuttling away.

Will held his breath. They were large. He had never seen lizards coloured so richly before. *Would they harm him?* Will knew he couldn't run, having barely managed to get this far. He waited.

The lizards pattered quickly up to his feet and stopped. Their pink eyes examined him carefully and then, turning together, they pattered away. The sound of their footsteps was just like his dream! Will grinned, or tried to. *That had to explain the footsteps, then.* But did it explain the smear of gold on his brow?

Will knew that if he was to keep his joints from locking, he would have to keep moving. Thirst was so all-consuming in his thoughts that he wondered whether it would drive him mad. He had heard once, long ago somewhere, that thirst made people lose their minds. He didn't want to find out if it were true.

He approached a corner in the laneway. The water sounded loudly. He wished he could run. Instead, he placed the Wand of Time harder into the ground and pushed his body on. Reaching past the corner, he was astonished to see a pair of ornate pillars forming an archway of intricate beauty. In the centre of the archway stood a small platform and on top of the platform, there was an urn. The urn drew its water from some unknown source, and then sent it trickling back down the platform to seep away. If Will's lips could have formed a shout, they would have. He hobbled garishly toward it.

Desperately reaching the archway, he let the Wand of Time drop to the ground. Plunging his face into the urn, Will slurped the water. It was the best thing he had ever tasted and he gulped, greedily.

He felt dizziness return, but steadied himself and then, having drunk enough, he began to slowly cleanse his wounds. His cramped fingers began to unlock, as the water's cool vigour brought life to them. Even the ever-present pain in his right knee began to grow fainter. In a flicker of new hope, he thought that perhaps at last he would be alright, that everything would be alright!

He stooped stiffly to pick up his wand, but to his surprise, she wasn't there. *Did he place her elsewhere?* Even as his eyes scoured the area, his heart sank. Too late, he noticed that the ground plunged sharply downhill. Grunting with the effort, Will stumbled into the centre of the laneway.

Rolling away, so far ahead that Will had no chance of catching her, the Wand of Time gathered momentum down the slope, to spin out of sight.

'Come back!' Will croaked, but the rainbow coloured walls muffled the words. He startled the lizards. They stared, bemused, and then scudded away.

It was all too much for Will. Without the wand, he knew pure defeat. Sitting down, he lowered his head into his hands. For no reason that he could understand, a bittersweet memory of Old came to him.

They were by a fireside in the forest. Old had offered Will a plain brown cup.

'What is it?' Will had asked.

'It is tea for sadness,' Old had replied.

Puzzled, Will had taken the cup. 'Tea for sadness?' he had questioned. 'What is tea for sadness?'

'Whatever you wish it to be,' Old had said, smiling.

Will looked up, his eyes full of memory. The blue lizards had returned and placed themselves by his feet, their pink eyes watching him closely.

Will stared back at them.

'Tea for sadness,' he whispered. 'I wish I had some now.'

CHAPTER 24

The Race

The Wand of Time rolled downwards, quickly gathering speed until she flurried so fast that a small pall of dust gathered in her wake. Even she had not expected this. She could do many things, but to stop rolling with the momentum of a hill was not one of them! For a time, she continued to hurtle through the laneway, until a twist in the passage sent her twirling over a lip of rock and into thin air. Finally, she dropped to the floor of an enormous cavern.

The force of the fall carried her along the cavern's floor where she collided into a wall. Bouncing off the wall as nimbly as rubber, she pivoted several times on her ends to finally land in a pocket of sand. A whoosh of air from a hole, high in the cavern's ceiling, pushed her into the sand and buried her there. The Wand of Time hummed, and then lay silent.

…

Rielle's eyes watered furiously from the speed of Benny's galloping. Grasping his mane as best as she could, she squinted ahead, surprising herself by staying on his back. She decided it was probably Benny who was making sure of that. Looking briefly down to check on Pud, she saw that her dog galloped with every sinew of his body, his ears pinned flat to his head.

Keeping abreast of the herd, Oobaat and Hope ran as easily and as fast as the unicorns. Rielle remembered that Old had also run like that. Clasping Benny's neck, she lowered herself closer to his body to stop the icy winds cutting her face. The thundering of the herd was deafening. The sound roared across the mountain.

...

With a heave and a flourish, the Sorcerer of Great Contempt pulled himself from the ocean and onto the shore. Triumphant, he threw the Staff of the Unimaginable into the air, catching her as she spun back down. His eyes pinned the spot on the mountain where the spiral of smoke sailed forth. He grinned. A message in the sky! What a timely gift. It told him exactly where he wanted to be. He reached out to the spot with a thought, but the thought was blocked. He tried again, holding the wand in both hands like an offering, but he could not get through.

'Protection!' he spat. 'A curse on Number Twenty Three!'

He squinted. A pall of dust billowed on the mountainside, far away. He threw his mind to it then stamped a foot and cursed.

'Traitors!' he screamed. 'I am free, do you hear me? I am free!'

A vision showed him that his brothers and the unicorns were thundering headlong, racing toward the smoke. Flinging from the shore, Neves On landed on the mountain's side. He tried to locate the spot from where the smoke spiralled, but it seemed that the mountain also had protection. He eyed the rough terrain.

'There's nothing for it,' he whispered to the unicorn wand. 'Primitive, yes, but it seems I, too, shall have to run.'

Grasping the white wand carefully, he went from a standstill to a gallop, and was coursing at a frightening speed in moments.

...

Hope and Oobaat glanced knowingly at each other.

'I can smell *his* evil!' Oobaat called. Hope nodded. With one thought, the herd and the group picked up speed. Impossibly, they ran faster.

Pud raced with everything he had. Staying by Benny's side, he looked up to check on his mistress from time to time.

Hurling along, clamped near Oobaat's armpit, little Bobs grinned. *He had been the one to spot the spiral of smoke.*

Jumping pot-holes, logs and rocks, the group powered on.

As Pud raced, he strangely remembered Old's golden parlour. The memory flared in his mind: a recollection of Old putting golden plates on a floor for him, then filling one with water and the other with cake.

In that moment, the mountain shook, fluffed itself, and belched loudly. The group galloped on despite the interruption, but then the mountain shook itself one more time with such ferocity that, although it didn't stop their headlong rush, it slowed everyone for several seconds.

As the mountain shook the first time, Pud was suspended in mid air and then, just as he landed, the mountain raised itself a second time and Pud tumbled briefly. Before he could clearly see where he was going, he careered to miss a boulder. Surprised, and in full flight, Pud hesitated briefly, and in the moment of doing so, he tripped. With a yelp, he felt himself falling. Before he quite understood what was happening, he realised that the dip in the ground was much more than just a pot hole.

Pud yowled but no one heard him above the sound of thundering hooves, as he fell hard and fast down into the depths of the mountain.

With her eyes almost closed against the biting wind, Rielle did not hear Pud's despairing calls. Instead, she heard someone whisper her name.

Rielle!

She bit her lip. 'Oh no,' she gasped, 'not my watcher again!'

…

Far and Flightlord grinned at each other.

'Friends?' Far chirped.

'Friends!' Flightlord chortled.

Turning to fly back into Hope's room, Far breathed a huge sigh of relief.

'A purple bottom suits you,' she chirped, 'and you never know, it might even be good for you to change colour now and then.' The remark was ludicrous and she knew it, but it sounded good. She slipped inside the tiny crack in the window. 'There must be some reason after all,' she continued, 'that Hope made the potion purple.

I mean,' she went on happily, 'there has to be a reason, don't you think? Hope is so wise and clever. I'm sure he wouldn't make it purple for no reason.'

The purple stain on the floor of Hope's room was still there where the empty bottle lay. Far flew down to it.

'Hmm,' she muttered, 'I'll have to clean this before Hope comes home.'

Fluttering around the mess on the floor, something caught her eye. She flew to the bottle and landed on it. Following the writing on the label with her feet, this time, she read the fine print. Far caught her breath and stifled a cry.

What had she done?

She contemplated the floor. Good, Flightlord hadn't drunk the entire potion. She grimaced. He had drunk quite a lot, though. She stood on tiptoe and tried to see him outside the window. He wasn't there. She wondered whether or not to tell him what was on the label. Shrugging her shoulders, she knew there was nothing for it but to tell the truth. Of course he would yell at her again, and perhaps this time, he might go away for good. She cringed at the thought and braced herself.

'Flightlord,' she called, but there was no answer.

She sighed with relief. That solved the problem for the moment. He was gone and she could tell him another day. A noise outside caught her attention. She planted her nose firmly against the window pane, looked around and down, then gasped. Climbing through the crack in the window, she flew outside.

'Flightlord!' she bellowed.

The rainbow dragon lay flat on his back with a smile on his face. He was fast asleep and snoring.

'Flightlord!' Far called again. He still didn't answer.

Far flew onto his nose and bit it as hard as she could. That usually woke him. Flightlord kept smiling and continued to snore.

Far hovered uncertainly for some moments, then flew wretchedly into the tower. She looked back and hung her head. She wondered if they could still be friends after this.

Flightlord was now purple, from head to tail!

...

Rana the frog, official substitute-watcher of the wishing pond, sighed with resignation. There was still no sign of Oobaat or the unicorns. Who would have thought that waiting could be so dull?

With new eyes, he looked carefully at the Tree of Life. All seemed well there. The white mist of the Ritual of Return poured richly from it, and now that Rana no longer took the tree for granted, his heart was warmed by the sight of it each day. Before the commotion in the forest, on the day that the tree had fought for dominion, Rana had been too self-interested to notice how different it was from the other trees.

He sighed again. Sometimes, he wished things could just return to the way they had been before... before his wish had come true and he had become the guardian to the pond. Sure, he'd wanted many things, and had hankered daily for what he thought those things could bring, but looking back, life had been so much simpler then. Oobaat had done all the real thinking and had made all the difficult decisions. It had meant that Rana could mostly do as he liked. Not any more though.

Oobaat's job as gatekeeper had looked so glamorous but things were not always what they seemed. Why couldn't hindsight, be foresight, Rana wondered. If he had to be truthful then he would admit that being gatekeeper was plain hard work, and hard work had never appealed to him. Half-heartedly, he ate a passing fly. Even the joy of catching flies on the wing did not have the same attraction as before, and he couldn't understand why.

After the Tree of Life had fought the invisible terror and won, things had returned to normal in the forest, except for two things. Hoot the great grey owl had become his friend, and to Rana's amazement, so had the ancient Imperial Guard snail, old Bobs.

At first Rana had been suspicious. Perhaps they were spying on him so that they could report to Oobaat when he returned. But Rana wasn't doing anything wrong, so that didn't make sense. Then he wondered whether they were planning to go to Wish, but it soon became clear that they had no intention of doing that. In the end, Rana gave up. Perhaps they simply liked him for who he was. Perhaps, at last, he had made new friends.

CHAPTER 25

Things you make they cannot break

Pud climbed the air as he fell, but it did no good; the air offered no footing and he continued to fall. He yowled, but he knew that the herd and Rielle would be long gone by now. Air rushed past as his fall took him deeply into the mountain. To see the ground was impossible, but as always, Pud hoped for the best. With a hard splash, he landed in icy water that sucked him down into deep, dark depths. He gulped and then remembered to keep his mouth shut, like the time he had travelled through the wishing pond to Wish.

Paddling furiously, he tried his best to surge upward, but the water held him under as if he were made of stone. He continued to sink. Finally, he hit what felt like the bottom, but when he tried to swim upward again, something seemed to be pressing solidly on his head. He couldn't push against it and he was growing short of breath.

To his right, a dim light pulsed, and so, instead of trying to swim upwards, he paddled sideways toward the light. As he swam, the light grew brighter. Pud paddled as fast as his exhausted legs would take him. Just as he thought he could not go on, he emerged on dry land. Gasping and coughing, he lay there. Some time went by. Eventually, Pud sat up. Looking around, he understood that he was very far from anyone or anything that he knew. His heart sank. Large chunks of crystal reflected off the water and the cave walls, sending out bright light by which he could see. He shook water from himself until he could shake no more, then found a patch of sand and rolled in it.

He was thirsty. Hesitantly, he turned and walked to the very water he had almost drowned in. As he drank, something flickered in the corner of his eye. Pud stood to attention, braced himself and growled. A strange dog was watching him! It was bright yellow and enormous. It growled back. Relieved, Pud saw that it wasn't the mottle-coated wolf.

Pud bristled. The yellow dog bristled. Nothing happened for a while. Pud furrowed his brow. Which dog would make the first move? The yellow dog frowned back, but that was all. Pud raised his lip and snarled; a deep, low sound in the back of his throat. The yellow dog snarled back. Pud stepped away to give himself space. The other dog also moved away. Quickly, Pud snapped around to confront him. There was no one there.

Squinting, Pud stepped gingerly back to the water's edge. The yellow dog came closer. Pud turned and looked over his shoulder. No one was there. Pud looked back into the water. The yellow dog was copying everything he did! But why? Pud winked one eye and the yellow dog winked back. Pud yawned and so did it. Pud scratched and the other dog scratched too. Finally, Pud had a thought.

Turning slowly and stretching his neck, he looked at his own back. It was bright yellow. Pud shook himself in disbelief, but the yellow didn't budge. He looked back at the water. He sat down and grinned. He was watching his own reflection; there was no one else there after all! Disappointment quickly followed his relief. A friend might have been handy down here in the bowels of the mountain. Why though, he wondered, was he bright yellow?

Turning from the water, he studied the enormous cavern. He peered up. Fresh air blasted and scrolled from a high hole in the cavern's roof and he wondered if that was where he had fallen from. It was a long way. Stalagmites decorated the area with interesting effect, and giant crystals lit the cavern almost like day. Pud sniffed the air. He knew one thing and one thing only: he must get back to the herd and Rielle.

He turned to look at his reflection. He didn't want to go back into the water, but he couldn't stay yellow. Grunting, he leapt in with a splash. Grimacing, he plunged and shook, hoping the yellow would wash away. Walking out, he looked in the water. It had worked! Black coat restored, he sauntered over to a patch of sand and rolled happily again.

As he rolled, Pud's foot tapped something buried in the sand. *Perhaps it was a bone!* Eagerly, Pud uncovered it. It wasn't a bone after all; it was just a long, yellow stick. Pud sighed. A bone to chew would have been even better than a friend in this lonesome place.

Relieved that he was black again, Pud turned to look smugly at his back. He was yellow again... it didn't make sense! The sand he stood on was quite golden but he had rolled in sand before. Pud shrugged and gave up. What difference did it really make? He was lost and far from the others. The urgency of finding them was far more important.

Nose held high, he sniffed. What would be the best way to leave the cavern? His paw bumped the stick again. This time, the stick made a noise. Pud leapt, surprised. He watched the spot for a moment, but nothing happened. Reaching with a tentative paw, he timidly touched the stick. It hummed. Pud pricked his ears. He had heard that sound before. Kinking his head to one side, he deliberately jabbed the stick, but harder this time. It hummed twice.

Eagerly, Pud dug away the sand surrounding the stick until it was fully exposed. He sat back and grinned. It was a stick just like the First Ones carried! He looked around. There were no First Ones here, though. He knew he had to find the others, but something told him he couldn't leave the stick behind. Pud scratched himself while he thought.

A sound and a new scent made Pud look up. A figure walked slowly toward him. Pud stood eagerly and wagged his tail. Someone had found him!

From the shadows, the figure emerged, walking toward Pud with one hand outstretched. In the other hand, the figure held a white walking wand.

Pud froze. Instinctively, he bared his teeth. The hackles on his neck rose stiffly. Number Seven of the First Ones stunk in Pud's nose. He was the evil one! *He had kidnapped his mistress once. He had sent the wolf to hurt her, and he was cruel to unicorns!* A growl formed deep in Pud's throat. Unsure, he stepped back.

The figure grinned. 'Good doggy,' it mocked, 'leave the nice stick for me now, there's a boy.' The Sorcerer of Great Contempt laughed mockingly.

'Ah,' he scorned, 'it seems that wonderful things come to those who wait. Not only freedom, but another wand!' He hooted, and the cavern echoed, helplessly. 'Not only will I now wield the unicorn wand but also the Wand of Time, if I'm not mistaken! What was it that little nobody, Eerht Ytnewt On used to say?' He paused, and stared seriously at Pud. *'Things I make, they cannot break when I hold the Wand of Time?'* The sorcerer scratched his chin. 'Something like that. Imagine, a world ruled by me, with all my power, unbroken, never broken, impossible to break! Imagine that!' He tore his eyes from Pud and looked greedily at the wand lying by the dog's feet. Neves On held out a hand.

Come to me Wand of Time
Come to me and now be mine!

Pud watched the sorcerer's hand shake with power, though the white wand in his other hand did not shine a light, or lend her strength. In front of Pud, the Wand of Time shifted and uttered a high note as if in protest, yet did not leap into Neves On's hand, as he had expected.

Pud wondered what to do. If the stick in front of him was the Wand of Time, then this must be where it had landed after Will had fallen to his tragic end.

Understanding in his heart told him that he was only a dog, but he could not allow the evil one to steal Will's wand. Old had given that wand to Will, and the wand must surely go back to Oobaat, or Hope, for safe keeping.

Defiantly, breaking all the laws of obedience written into the code of a dog's sinews and bones, Pud stepped forward and stood over the wand.

'Go!' roared Neves On. 'Go, or I will roast you alive, you buffoon!'

Pud watched the Wand of Time losing a battle of her own as she inched unwillingly toward the sorcerer. Sure of his prize, the sorcerer grinned.

Before he fully understood what he was doing, Pud grabbed the wand in his jaws. A tremendous shock of power from the Wand of Time rocked Pud's body, lifting him clean off the ground. In blinding moments which took his breath away, Pud astonishingly understood what it felt like to be human and also, something more! Landing back on his feet, Pud bolted, with the wand gripped firmly in his mouth.

Behind him, the Staff of the Unimaginable glowed white at her centre and sang a note that chimed to the ceiling.

'Come back!' the sorcerer roared.

But Pud had already slipped from the cavern. Galloping faster than he'd ever done, the last thing Pud saw was the look of disbelief on Neves On's face.

CHAPTER 26

Fly like a bird leave life behind ...
Wounded and bruised please take me home

Will held a battered hand out to the blue lizards but they scampered. 'Don't go,' he pleaded gruffly, 'I'm a friend.' But they were gone.

Feeling terribly alone, the dark times of Will's past began to seem almost endurable. Loneliness closed bleakly over his heart. His wounds felt better after bathing them, but in his loss, he was barely grateful. To be without the Wand of Time was unbearable. He hated himself for the times he had not wanted her. She was gone now, and who knew where? Doubt crowded his thoughts.

Could he ever move forward again?

A gentle glow lit the pathway, almost as if the moon shone through the cave somehow, but that was ridiculous. Will knew he was buried in the depths of the mountain. Was it night or day outside? Was the sun shining, perhaps?

Forgetful, he reached for the walking wand, but instantly, his heart blamed him for her loss. He wanted to weep. The lizards, he noticed keenly, had not returned.

Should he move on?

His right knee could now bend a little, but hunger cramped his stomach. He rose slowly and drank from the urn in an attempt to fill his belly. Too unsure of his next move, he settled himself in the alleyway again.

Memories began to tickle the corners of his thoughts. Flashes of the past crept and then galloped by him, until his mind was too full to bear. Anguish gripped him.

He could not blame anyone else for the way things had turned out, or the mess he was in. Arrogantly, he had charged the shores of Wish so very, very long ago, to claim a unicorn horn. He grimaced. How young and ignorant he had been! Did he really believe all that time ago, that it was his right to wish for *anything?* He shifted uncomfortably. He had met evil that day, and it had not left him since. He had also met Candela.

Will rose and sipped from the urn in an effort to distract himself. He tried to send the memories away, but they twirled like drifting autumn leaves that would not fall to ground.

He thought of the butterfly, Far, on the day she had set him free from being a shrub. She had been rude and belligerent toward him. It was exactly what he had deserved. But evil had dogged his new-found freedom, despite the First Ones and the unicorns being so good to him.

Will winced with the futile longing that somehow he could change the past. Everything he did was wrong! Old had entrusted him with a walking wand, an honour for any human, let alone for someone like him, and now, even she was gone. He sighed and sat down. He closed his eyes.

Will remembered a conversation held shortly after the

battle in the almond orchard. Their group had reached Old's mountain and they were resting after their ordeal. He had been preoccupied and, like everyone else, grief stricken. Hope had come to sit near him. Will had turned to him.

'Don't you feel bad that Old took the wand from you before she exploded?' Will had asked Hope, rudely.

Hope had looked kindly at him before answering, his eyes thoughtful and warm.

'We all make choices,' he had replied quietly, 'and Number Twenty Three had his reasons for doing what he did.' Hope had paused. 'Perhaps,' he went on, 'perhaps he needed to pass the wand on to you, and that was the best way he knew how.'

Will had frowned, shocked. 'What a ridiculous thing to say,' he had argued, 'why would he do that?'

Hope had shifted and placed a quiet hand on Will's shoulder.

'Perhaps,' he had murmured, his eyes boring into Will's, 'perhaps he wanted certain things from you.'

Will had made a face of disbelief. 'What things?' he'd spat.

Hope had stood, looking thoughtfully at Will. He began to step away, but then paused and turned back.

'He wanted you to be brave, Will, and to face your fear. He wanted you to tell yourself the truth. Above all, he wanted you to do the right thing.'

Will had been dumbfounded, but before he could answer, Hope had gone.

With strangled rage, Will had growled. 'What do you know? What do any of you know?' Spitefully, he had kicked dirt at the Wand of Time.

Will groaned. Like a drifting leaf, more memories floated in.

He had told Rielle the truth; he had told her all his secrets on the night they had hidden from the wind storm, in the Valley of Possibility. Rielle had not judged him or withdrawn her friendship, despite the things he had told her. She had remained exactly the same, a true friend.

Will sighed. He wondered if he should continue down the laneway and through the mountain, but before he could move, another memory hurtled with startling force and clarity around the corners of his mind.

He had stayed alone that first night on the mountain, stricken at the loss of Old. Thoughts of the battle in the almond orchard had overwhelmed him. He had held the Wand of Time as if she were at fault. Despising her, he had wanted to fling her away. He had wanted to turn to the others and tell them he was going home, and that they could find Old's caves without him.

In the middle of his thoughts, Rielle had come to stand by him. She had brought him tea for sadness and some cake from Old's golden cake tin. Will had flinched at her kindness and had almost hated her for daring to offer it.

Didn't anyone realise that it was because of him that Old was dead? It was because of him that Candela had almost been killed? That it was because of him the sorcerer was able to come so close to them all?

Without a word, Rielle had held the cake and tea out to him. Behind her own dire grief, she had tried her best to smile.

'Go away,' Will had yelled at her, 'leave me alone!'

Rielle had stood uncertainly, in disbelief.

Will had glared. 'Are you still here?' he had sneered.

Cruelly, he had watched her fight new tears. She had tried to look as if his words had not hurt her, that they had not mattered.

'I wanted to be sure you were alright,' she had finally stammered. 'I've been worried about you. You look lonely. I thought you might like some company. Are you sure you want me to go?'

Deliberately, Will had turned his back on her. 'I said so, didn't I?' he retorted.

'But,' she had persisted, standing her ground, 'I... I thought we were friends, Will? I know you're hurt and frightened, but you don't have to hide from me.'

Will had turned and thrown her a hate-filled look. How dare she be so nice to him! How dare she be kind to a villain like him!

'Go away,' he had growled.

'Don't be like this, Will,' Rielle had answered crossly, 'I thought we were good friends!' Her resolve had failed then. She had choked on the next words. 'Aren't we?'

Ignoring her, Will had thrown his hat down. Getting up, and not looking back, he had stomped away. But he had seen the look in her eyes.

'I don't need anybody,' he'd snarled.

Something had rustled close by. Afraid, Will had stopped.

Candela was there, with watchful eyes. 'You don't need anybody, Willful James?' she had whispered. 'No man is a world of his own, Will.'

Will had said nothing. He wanted to storm off, but respect for the unicorn had kept his feet still.

Candela had taken a step closer. 'You push away those who care. Why do you do that?' She had paused. 'Don't you know,' she had continued, 'don't you know that love is the greatest gift of all?'

Will had sneered. 'No one loves me! No one cares about me!'

Candela had stepped even closer. Will was forced to look at her whether he wanted to or not. She had stared steadily at him until his eyes dropped. When she answered, her voice was stern.

'Be careful,' she had cautioned. 'In the past you confused truth and friendship with things that were not. Now, when you are safe to trust, you refuse, at great cost.'

A vision of the Sorcerer of Great Contempt had flashed into Will's thoughts, but perplexed, he had pushed it to the back of his mind.

Despite Will's growing impatience, Candela had continued.

'Flightlord and Far took you to Hope when you almost died. Do you remember that? They asked nothing in return. What about Hope? Hope cares about you as he cares for all mankind.'

Will had still said nothing.

Candela had tossed her head. Unusually impatient, she was growing tired of the young man.

'The dog loves you,' she had trilled on a lighter note, hoping he might laugh or at least, smile.

'Pud loves everyone!' Will had retorted.

'No, that's where you're wrong.' Candela had sighed, on the verge of giving up. 'The dog loves with a clever heart.'

Will had grown increasingly more restless and uncomfortable. Candela had pitied his discomfort; Will could see it in her eyes.

Candela had looked quizzically at him. 'Do you know the riddle of unicorns, Willful James?'

Will had stared insolently at her. 'What do you mean?' Her questioning had aggravated him. 'I've never heard of it.'

Candela had nodded. 'Well then, that explains a lot.' She

was quiet for a while and Will had grown restless.

'Perhaps,' Candela had finally stated, 'instead of pushing Rielle away, like you just cruelly did, perhaps you might like to ask her what the riddle of unicorns is.'

Will had sighed with exaggerated annoyance. 'Why would I ask her that? She follows me around fussing, keeping her sneaky eyes on me all the time. She probably reports, to the others, the things that I do. I just want to be left alone.'

'Because,' Candela had snapped, sick of his silly games, 'because she has gone before you. Not long ago, she too was forced to walk alone, until she was shown the meaning of the riddle. She has been a true friend to you. You just have to believe it.'

'What's so wrong with walking alone?' Will had snapped back, half ignoring what she'd said. 'At least if things go wrong, you only have yourself to blame!' He went to walk away.

Candela hadn't finished. 'Why do you punish yourself, Willful James? Until you stop, you will punish everyone around you.'

Will had frowned. What in blazes was she going on about? Punish himself? Why would he do that? He had said nothing.

Candela had continued. 'What about Oobaat? What about the herd? We all care about you, Will. Have you already forgotten Eerht ytnewt On? If he hadn't cared, why then, tell me this… why would he have given you the Wand of Time? Do you know what a privilege that is? Not many humans even get to see one, let alone become a wand's custodian.'

Candela had been tiring of him; Will could see that.

'Hmm,' she had breathed, 'hmm, perhaps you are more like Number Twenty Three of the First Ones, than you think.'

'What do you mean?' Will gasped. 'I'm nothing like Old!'

Candela had looked piercingly at him and this time, Will could not look away.

'Aren't you Willful James?' she whispered. 'What about your power?'

Will's chin had jerked up. 'I have power?' he had exclaimed.

Candela had watched him placidly. It had made him uneasy.

'Humility,' she had finally responded, 'you lack humility, Willful James... you always have.' Turning sharply, and without another word or look, she had cantered from his sight.

Confused, Will had stood for a long while. What did she mean, he lacked humility? First she had told him that he was more like Old than he imagined and then she had told him he lacked humility! How could he and Old be similar, then? Old had not only been wise and powerful, kind and strong, but most of all he had been humble. Will grimaced. That proved he was nothing like Old!

Walking back to the group, he had picked a small yellow wildflower that grew tenaciously on the hard-bitten mountainside. Without a word, he had gone to where Rielle sat and placed it on the rock beside her.

Rielle had looked doubtfully at him. 'I thought you didn't like me?' she glared.

'I never said that,' Will had responded uncomfortably.

Rielle had stood up. 'Just a while ago, you didn't need anyone, especially my friendship.'

'I... I thought you'd like the flower,' he'd stammered.

Rielle had frowned. 'I don't like the way you behave!' She had walked away and left him standing there, and had gone to *sit with the others.*

Will's resentment had flared. He was right. He couldn't trust anyone, not even her! But in the last look she had given him, he knew he had broken her heart. He'd pushed the thought aside. Looking down, he'd noticed that the flower was gone.

The memory crushed Will. As if awakening from a dream, he remembered where he was: in the depths of a mountain, lost and alone.

Oddly, a rhyme and a tune flowed through his thoughts, and Will began to hum. The tune was catchy, and despite his plight, Will felt his heart had turned a corner.

A strange sight in the lonely mountain corridor, Will began to sing.

Magic happens when I surrender
And face the hardship of nature's shores
When I bleed in the embrace of Angels
And lay helpless in their arms

When I'm lost and blinded by the light
And find greater comfort in the night

Magic happens when I surrender
And all I cherish is lost and gone
When my clothes are rags and my bones lay freezing
And I curse with rage at all that's wrong

When I'm lost and blinded by the light
And find greater comfort in the night

Magic happens when I surrender
And all the doors are broken or closed
When every time I find some shelter
There's no roof to hide the snow

When I'm lost and blinded by the light
And find greater comfort in the night

Magic happens when I surrender
And walk naked, shoeless, hatless, and laugh
When I find a mirror watching me
Reflecting my soul, reflecting my heart

When I'm lost and blinded by the light
And know at last that it's all right

Magic happens when I surrender
And find the love I always wanted was locked inside me all along
Locked inside me with the light
Locked inside to guide me home

When Angel's arms no longer claim me
But let me walk with care, alone.

Will cringed again and shut his eyes. How horribly he had treated everyone! He could see now that they had all been looking out for him. He had been so ungrateful, angry, and even spiteful. If there was the slightest chance he would ever leave this confounded place, then he must find the others, and apologise. He had to make amends for his behaviour. Rielle's face shone in his mind. A tear squeezed from his closed eyes. He had distrusted her friendship and loyalty, and judged her motives wrongly.

A sudden noise in the passageway made Will turn and look. A huge yellow dog was watching him, and in its mouth, it held a wand, the colour of honey wood!

CHAPTER 27

The rite of passage

The sound of thundering hooves boomed across the mountain. Rielle glanced down. Pud wasn't there! A rapid glimpse over her shoulder proved that he was nowhere in sight. The herd was galloping with such conviction that no one had noticed. Rielle leaned close to Benny's ear to cry out.

Rielle...

They all heard the call, and in a split second, the herd and the First Ones stopped in full flight, sending dust to churn and roll around them in a billowing brown cloud.

Hope immediately went to Rielle. 'Your watcher calls,' he whispered, 'we *must* know what it means this time.' The herd instantly closed ranks and stood facing outward, each pair of eyes and ears alert.

Rielle swung from Benny's back. She gasped and clutched her brow. As she touched her star-scar, vivid pictures flashed through her mind.

Hope placed an urgent hand on her shoulder. 'What is it?' he demanded.

As clearly as if she were there, Rielle watched pictures

form in her mind's eye. Before she even had a chance to wonder about it, the visions scrolled on.

Pud! She saw him fall down a hole that plunged him into the mountain's depths, and then watched him roll in golden sand which made him yellow. She began to sigh with relief that he was alright, but then, horrified, she watched him turn and face the Sorcerer of Great Contempt.

Rielle seized Hope's arm as the vision gripped her. She watched the sorcerer say something but she couldn't hear what it was. He reached out a gnarled hand and yelled something at Pud. Pud grabbed what looked like a walking wand in his mouth and then, in a daring dash, he turned and ran. She watched Pud speed through a long, beautiful passageway, his breath rasping from the effort. Rielle cried out. She couldn't believe what she was seeing. Pud had stopped. There was someone else in the passage!

Hope reached out and took her arms to steady her. With unwavering strength, Rielle gathered herself and turned to the group.

'Pud is with Will!' she cried.

'How is that so?' Coraggio asked, stepping forward.

'I... well, I just *saw* it,' Rielle whispered, white-lipped. 'I mean, I noticed that Pud wasn't with us just a second before my, er, *watcher* called, and then, for some reason I can't explain, my star-scar felt hot.'

She looked helplessly at Hope as if worried that no one would believe her, or that she might not believe herself.

'And now... well, now, I just had a... I just had a *vision*,

I suppose,' she finished quietly, hoping they would understand. 'I mean, well, what I mean, is that I just saw all these things happening as clearly as if I were there.'

Hope looked keenly at her. 'Has this happened before?' he urged.

Coraggio, Candela and Oobaat stepped closer to Rielle. Their eyes pressed eagerly for her answer.

Rielle looked around at their waiting faces. She shook her head.

'No, not like this.' She frowned. 'I mean, I've sometimes dreamed of things that later came true, but... well... but, no, I've never done this before.' She stared pensively at the unicorns and the First Ones. 'This is the kind of thing that *you* all do,' she murmured, wondering if she should be concerned. 'It's not the kind of thing that I normally do is it?' She tried to grin. 'I mean, I'm just an ordinary human girl.'

The leaders of the group exchanged quick glances.

Rielle remembered something. She gasped.

'What is it?' the others urged.

'*He's* here!' she cried. 'I just remembered; I saw him too!'

The group stirred. They didn't need to ask whom she meant.

'Ah, your watcher tells us *this!*' Coraggio exclaimed.

Oobaat paced up and down then stopped and whirled around.

'So! Neves On has most definitely escaped from Wish. At last, we know for sure!'

Although disturbed by the vision, Rielle sighed with relief.

'So you believe me?' she interrupted.

'Believe you?' Oobaat frowned. 'Of course we believe

you! Why in blazes wouldn't we?'

Rielle shook her head. 'Well, it's just strange that I'm the one who should have seen these things.'

Silence clutched the group. Small tufts of wind plucked the leaves of bushes and created jingles from the rustling sounds.

Hope looked kindly at Rielle. He picked his words carefully, his voice becoming wistful.

'You held the Wand of Faith, young Rielle, and what is more, she sang for you. Somehow, somewhere, your heart and her knowledge met.' He nodded knowingly at her. 'You will never be the same again.'

Rielle could have sworn his eyes twinkled, despite everything.

Hope smiled at her puzzled expression. 'It could not have happened if the wand herself had not chosen it. But we will talk more another time,' he finished quickly. 'We must decide what to do now.'

'Was it definitely Will that you saw?' Benny pressed.

Rielle nodded. 'Yes, but for some strange reason, Pud had what looked like a walking wand in his mouth, and Will didn't seem to have a wand at all... and... they faced each other as if they didn't know each other, and Pud had just run away from the... the sorcerer, through all these laneways that seem to be down there.' She looked at the ground and then looked back up, her cheeks flushed. 'I have no idea what it all means!'

'Don't panic,' Candela soothed, 'although it looks bad, it might be better than we think.' She paused. 'What do you mean, Pud had a *wand?*'

Rielle frowned at the memory. 'For some reason Pud

had what looked like a walking wand in his mouth... a honey coloured one just like Will's.' She chewed her lip, remembering. 'In the brief moment I saw Will, he wasn't holding the Wand of Time.'

Oobaat held a hand up for everyone's attention. 'Enough conjecture... we have no time, there is no time. It is enough to know Rielle has had this timely vision. Now we must decide how to act upon it.' He turned and looked thoughtfully at Rielle. 'If what you tell us is accurate, then Will and the dog are in extreme peril.' He glanced pensively around.

'Somewhere in the depths of this mountain our greatest enemy walks freely, and at any moment for all we know, he may find Old's gold and uncover its secrets. If he should catch up with Will and Pud, then they are....' He stopped speaking. His expression was enough.

An idea crossed Oobaat's thoughts. He turned to Rielle.

'Was Will in good spirits?' he asked urgently. 'Did he look well?'

Rielle frowned, casting her mind to the fleeting image of Will. Her eyes opened wide and she shook her head quickly.

'He looked like death,' she whispered unhappily. 'He, well, he was covered in cuts and bruises and he could barely stand.'

The unicorns and Hope murmured loudly at the news.

'And Pud?' Oobaat pressed.

Rielle brightened. 'No, I'm almost sure Pud was fine, but....'

Oobaat scowled. 'Out with it, but what?'

Rielle took no offence at his abrupt manner. 'Pud was

bright yellow,' she said, pulling a face.

Perhaps it wasn't a vision after all. Why would her black dog be yellow?

To her surprise, the herd and the First Ones gasped.

'The golden sands,' Candela rushed the words.

The herd trilled loudly.

'What?' Rielle cried. 'What does that mean?'

Hope grasped her shoulder. 'It means, young Rielle, that we must hurry. The chances are that Pud is covered in the golden sands.'

Rielle opened her mouth to speak, but Hope went on.

'According to one conversation we had with Number Twenty Three, the golden sands are not real gold, just some fun he had with time on his hands. But it means that wherever you saw Will and Pud, they must be very close to the real thing.' He took a deep breath. 'They must be close to finding Old's caves.'

In the brief hush, Rielle reluctantly knew something.

'The sorcerer was in the place of the golden sands,' she muttered. Horrified, she stared helplessly at Hope. 'Does that mean he is also close to finding Old's caves?'

The silence that followed her words was so deep that even the flicker of breeze stopped. From the frozen moment, and from what appeared to be thin air, a large black bird appeared. With a clap of wings that sounded like thunder in the silence, it landed close by, to stare at them.

No one moved.

Rielle's first reaction was to reach for Pud, but of course, he wasn't there.

'It's the sorcerer!' little Bobs cried out.

Oobaat stepped in front of the young snail and kindly held a finger to his mouth. Oobaat stood, and with the others, waited. Nothing moved or made a sound for what seemed a very long time.

Rielle held her breath.

Was this the sorcerer? Was he once again disguised? It was the same bird she had seen on the ledge where Will's hat had been! Perhaps she should have said something, then? Was it the sorcerer? Was it Neves On?

Candela finally stepped forward and spoke for all of them.

'What say you, crow?' she boldly asked.

The crow blinked yellow eyes at her and bobbed its head, but then it turned and looked directly at Rielle.

'*Rielle*,' it croaked, 'I am here for you.'

Rielle gasped. *It was the voice of her watcher!* She glanced at Hope and Benny. She could see they knew it too.

It didn't make sense. If this was the sorcerer, then why did he bother to send a warning each time some upheaval was about to happen? Rielle thought back. The crow could not possibly be Neves On. The voice had been following her since before she had met Old. A horrible thought crossed her mind. Maybe it was the sorcerer? Maybe, just like poor Will, evil had been stalking her for the longest time. But why? What had she done?

And then, in a moment of clarity, Rielle thought she understood. She took a deep breath. She felt lost without faithful Pud by her side, yet bravely, looking neither left nor right, she stepped forward to meet the crow.

Valiant dog with amber eyes

Dumbfounded, Will and Pud faced each other. Will saw a huge yellow apparition of a dog, with curled lips and bared teeth, holding what looked like the Wand of Time. With heaving sides and his ears pinned to his head, Pud involuntarily grimaced as he clamped the wand in his mouth.

Will frowned. It couldn't be! Looking closely, he saw that the yellow on the dog was splotchy at best, and that underneath, a dark coat shone. Could it be?

Amazed, Pud realised that the battered and bruised wreck of a human before him was Will. The revelation was a welcome one. Placing the wand gently on the ground, Pud pranced, overjoyed.

'Pud?' Will croaked.

Pud sneezed. Picking the wand up once again, he received a jolt from her touch, but he recovered quickly. Carefully, he placed the wand into one of Will's poor, ruined hands. Will's heart swelled. His swollen fingers closed firmly around the wand. Although his right knee complained bitterly, he kneeled and held the dog closely.

'Pud,' Will stammered gruffly, 'it's good to see you, boy!'

Pud understood that terrible things had happened to Will, so he stood patiently for him.

'Are the others with you?' Will questioned eagerly, looking over Pud's shoulder with a longing beyond all longing, to see his friends. 'Is Rielle here too? Are they all here with you?' His voice was almost its usual self. 'Where are they boy?' He wanted to laugh with relief. 'Are they following you?' Joy filled Will's heart so thoroughly at the thought of being reunited that he stood easily, as if nothing hurt.

Brief scuttling sounds in the passageway made Will and Pud turn. Convinced the dog was not alone, Will walked almost nimbly to meet the sounds. His mind's eye could see them all; their dear, trusted faces flashed before him, as he did his best to hurry.

'Hello?' he called, willing them to him. Will looked down for Pud to share the moment but Pud had stopped. Instead, he stood with hackles raised, like a statue of distress.

Will faltered and his heart froze. Small hairs on the back of his neck prickled. His grip tightened on the Wand of Time, and then, he knew. He quivered and closed his eyes, his mind recoiling, his gut churning.

He was not ready.

'Willful James,' whispered the voice that Will remembered so well.

Will squeezed his eyes tightly shut and controlled a short sob in his throat.

Would he never be free? Would they all never be free of this affliction?

Will gripped the walking wand so tightly that the new scabs forming on his fingers cracked, broke and bled. He didn't notice. Panic was his taskmaster and fear was his curse.

'Hello, Willful James.' A rush of cold blasted the corridor and a laugh, though soft, echoed like a pall.

Pud snarled. Will heard something strike the dog hard. Pud screeched. Silence followed. It was the silence that broke Will's indecision. He opened his eyes. Pud lay, barely breathing.

Anger bubbled and burst through Will's thick wall of terror. Rage rose to conquer the sob in his throat. He faced Neves On, Number Seven of the First Ones, the Sorcerer of Great Contempt. In that moment, Will knew there was no going back now. Not ever!

Casually, Neves On prodded Pud's still form with the Staff of the Unimaginable. A dark score on the wand glowed red as he did so. Promptly, he shifted the way he held her and was relieved that she did not bite him. He looked up, straight through Will's eyes and beyond. His lip curled.

'I haven't killed the creature yet,' he leered, 'but he has interfered too many times, you must understand.'

Will swore under his breath. Painfully, he did his best to stand on his aching right leg. 'Would you maim or kill an innocent creature?' he growled.

The sorcerer raised an eyebrow. 'I?' he laughed. 'Me?' he jeered. 'And who was it that wanted a unicorn horn, once long ago, and would have done anything for such a treasure?' He laughed abrasively and seared Will with such a look of dark contempt that Will flinched, and was tempted to give up then, knowing it was true.

Pud twitched and groaned.

Will knew that if by some lucky chance he would ever see Rielle again, then he must do everything in his power to save her treasured dog. Gripping the wand that Old had given him with faith and determination, he took a deep breath and carefully exhaled.

'That,' he replied, 'was a very, very long time ago. I am not that boy now. I've changed. I'm not that person anymore.' Will paused. Fury gripped his stomach. Something inside him snapped. 'Anyway,' he spat, 'you have what you wanted. You have your freedom. Why don't you leave me alone? You don't need me to do your dirty work any more. Just leave me alone and go and do whatever it is that someone like you, does!'

Neves On roared with laughter at Will's boldness.

'Do you think you can really change?' he sneered. 'Ha! Do you think you can escape me, or what you are? Do you really believe that you can be free?' He squinted. 'You don't believe in yourself or even *like* yourself, Willful James, so tell me, what, or whom, do you intend to change into? Do you think that you can escape me? You *are* me! You and I inhabit the same place, Willful James. You can never be rid of me! Never!'

In that terrifying moment, Will's mind closed around the words, believing them so thoroughly that darkness flooded him like a wave of foul, chilling water. The old fear gripped his stomach, clutching it into knots that wouldn't let him breathe. Leaning with all his weight into the Wand of Time, he accidentally jolted her. She hummed and the sound nudged him from his stupor. He glanced up to see a look of amazement in Neves On's eyes.

'How is it,' the sorcerer asked with deadly softness, 'how is it that the wand hums for *you*?' He waited, eyes fixed, for Will's reply.

Will flinched as if he had been hit. Could it be that the powerful monster before him did not know that Old had given him the walking wand?

In Will's mind, the moment of Old handing him the wand was so clear and ever-present that it never occurred to him that the sorcerer could not know. The realisation gave him a surge of fleeting power. He paused before answering and a glimmer of cunning flooded his senses. For a while at least, he held the surprise card.

'Answer me!' bellowed the sorcerer. The white wand in his hand flared red at her centre and she bit him twice. Neves On held back a humiliated gasp. Enough of her insolence! Infuriated by her constant betrayal, he gathered dark dust and thoughts about himself until Will could barely see for the blanket of corruption that surrounded them.

In a need to punish, to hurt and to maim, Neves On knew he could not risk harming the wand he held, although the anger and hatred he bottled within was spurred on and fuelled by her treachery. *He deserved loyalty from the unicorn wand!* It was *he* who wielded *her*, not the other way around. Thwarted, angry and humiliated, he flung a projectile of vile anger and bitterness toward Will.

The Wand of Time streamed a high note of warning.

With a decision that would have made Old proud, Will knew he must act. At first, it was just a feeling, a gut feeling, a fleeting intuition and a tickling of his senses. He knew something he was unwilling to accept before. Despite his clumsy body, almost effortlessly, he knew what to do.

Will side-stepped the thrust of solid anger from the sorcerer, and tapping the Wand of Time to the ground, he thought himself away. No sooner was the thought formed than it was done! Will's senses reeled. He was standing behind Neves On!

So, this was how it felt to take charge of a walking wand!

Will could not believe that he had finally done it, but there was no time to reflect now. He had to manage a way of escape, for himself and the dog.

Whirling to meet Will's action, the sorcerer screeched with frustration.

'Impossible,' he roared, 'the wands are made for First Ones! No human can wield them! What trickery is this?'

Will almost laughed at Neves On's confusion, but events had taught him to fight to the bitter end. *Triumph wasn't his yet.* He stood taller, and this time, he deliberately touched the wand he held. The Wand of Time hummed.

Maddened beyond belief, Neves On cunningly changed tack. His face became a mask of blank non-resistance.

'How is it you wield this wand? Tell me, why can you make her sing? Did you steal her from my dying brother?' He swore. 'No, the others would never have let you do such a thing.' He sucked his breath sharply. 'It can only mean one thing. Eerht ytnewt On, my brother, *gave* you the wand you hold, didn't he? He gave you the Wand of Time to make your own.'

Will said nothing. Fear almost overcame him. His mind raced toward his next move.

Neves On stroked his chin. 'Not only did he give you the wand,' he reflected, 'but he must have told you about his gold.' A slow smear stretched his darkened lips. He raised and pointed the white wand at Will. 'Tell me where the gold is, Willful James. Tell me now or face my power.'

The Staff of the Unimaginable flared in her centre.

Will knew that no matter who had made her, the sorcerer wielded the white wand and for him she must work. He trembled. He had seen the destruction done on the morning of the battle of the almond orchard. He had watched Old die at the hands of the powerful, corrupt villain standing before him. He would never forget. Afraid, yet still too unsure of his own abilities, Will tried to play for time.

'I'm curious,' Will asked, working to keep his voice steady, 'why it is you want Old's gold? You have your freedom and you hold the most powerful walking wand ever made. Why does someone like you need some bits of gold?'

The sorcerer snorted derisively. 'Some bits of gold, you say? Are you pretending? Surely you know what this gold means?'

Will's leg hurt. Sweat began to stain his brow, dripping into his eyes and marring his vision. His mind screamed for an escape, yet he knew he could not leave Pud behind.

Specks of blood spattered the Wand of Time from the bleeding wounds on his hands. For the moment, he was trapped. But he needed to know about Old's gold. He needed to know why it was so important to everyone.

After their group had left Wish, Will had kept apart from the others. Too absorbed with self pity and anger, he had not listened to the unicorns and the First Ones talk.

'Tell me about Old's gold,' Will prompted quietly, almost as if he were making polite conversation.

Neves On barked a laugh as if he understood now that Will was bluffing his way through; that Will didn't know everything a bearer of a walking wand should know.

'Eerht ytnewt On,' began the Sorcerer of Great Contempt in a velvet tone, 'devoted the last few thousand years to this mountain we stand in.' Sneaking a derisive peek at Will, he still pointed the white wand at his throat. 'Number Twenty Three decided to discover the meaning of all things, and how it was that life existed.' He glared at Will with such envy and greed in his eyes that Will flinched. 'While I was locked in exile in Wish, he was busy doing what I should have achieved, don't you see?'

Will nodded just to agree, but it occurred to him that if the sorcerer had really wanted such a thing, he could have done it in Wish. He had the power, and although he had been stripped of holding a wand, surely, instead of brooding and hating, he might have done something more useful with his time? Will quickly refocused on what was being said.

Neves On continued. 'Eerht Ytnewt On discovered the formula to *life*. That *nobody*, discovered how to create and to transform matter; how to change the very substance of stuff! With his plodding, dull ways, he learned how to turn the dirt of this mountain into pure, perfect gold.'

'I see,' Will said, although he really didn't see at all. 'You want his gold so you can become rich? Is that how you'll have the power you want?'

Neves On glared so harshly that Will shook.

'You humans,' the sorcerer spat, 'you think everything revolves around worldly goods! Don't you know anything? Didn't you hear a word I just said?' He paused and resumed speaking in a quieter tone.

'Number Twenty Three knew the formula to *life!* He could fashion things from *nothing*, or change how things were, and turn them… into something else! Don't you see? Don't you understand?'

Will thought he was beginning to see.

'Listen to me Willful James. Listen! Eerht ytnewt On knew the formula to *life*… he knew the *formula.*' The sorcerer paused and his eyes became mere slits. The wand he held wavered. 'He knew the formula to eternal life!' Neves On breathed deeply as if the excitement of even saying the words was too good to be true. He sneered at the uncertainty in Will's face, before finishing with a grimace. 'He knew the formula to *eternal* life, and with that wand you hold in your hands, the Wand of Time, he could make things last *forever!*'

Will reeled. He finally understood. The sorcerer wanted to live even longer than the thousands of years already allotted to First Ones! He wanted to wield the ultimate power of the unicorn wand, for all time, unchallenged, with control over everything that was known. Will felt sick. He could barely find his voice.

'If Old knew the formula to eternal life,' Will whispered, 'then how is it he was killed in the battle of the almond orchard? Why wasn't he revived?'

The sorcerer leaned closer to Will and sneered. 'Because he was a humble fool! Instead of choosing to make himself powerful, he tinkered with making bits of mountain turn to gold. He built his silly bridge which I managed with the greatest accident of luck to destroy, but it was only luck. He built his useless walls and tinkered with bits of stone and crystal, but he did nothing useful with all his knowledge, dullard that he was.'

The Wand of Time shifted slightly in Will's grasp and her centre light glowed, even as she twanged a discordant note.

The Sorcerer of Great Contempt grinned at her discomfort.

'Somewhere in this place,' he breathed, with a catch of excitement in his throat, 'is *the formula*, the one true formula that will soon belong to me.' He pinned Will with ambitious eyes.

Will recognised that look. He began to back away.

Neves On roared with laughter.

'You can't escape me, Will,' he hissed. 'I have another task for you now, my friend. You are going to find that formula for me. You are still of use to me.'

Will shook his head. More than anything, he wanted to be healthy in his body at that moment, for he knew that he had never in his entire life been sounder in his mind.

'No,' Will whispered, 'no, this time I will not do your dirty work. I am a different person now. You don't control me anymore. You are *not* me and I am *not* you. I won't do anything else for you. Not now. Not ever. You will have to kill me first.'

Neves On stepped closer to Will. Nearby, Pud jerked and moaned.

'Until you have looked death in the eye, Willful James,' the sorcerer hissed ominously, 'you have not been invited to live!' He paused and glared. 'So, look... look now and choose!'

In that moment, Will knew a spark of a different fear. Could he use the wand again? Had the first time, just minutes ago, been nothing but luck? Could he draw and use that strength of knowing and purpose, deep inside his heart and mind, once more? In a flash of truth, he realised it was doubt that had stopped him using her power all along. Doubt that had perhaps changed the course of the journey up the mountain to find Old's gold. Because of doubt, he, and he alone, may have changed the fate of his dear friends; friends who had stuck by him and shown him nothing but goodness, despite his selfish moods and uncaring ways.

In one swift movement, despite his bruised and broken body, Will scooped the huge dog into his arms, tapped the Wand of Time to the ground, and thought himself away.

It worked! In a searing moment, he stood on a mountain outcrop that faced a large opening into the mountain itself. A wall ran along a pathway made of stone and rock, carefully built and well tended. Below the wall, a valley spread peacefully into the distance.

Will placed Pud carefully beside the sanctuary of the wall. Pud whined and woke. The dog's eyes looked to

Will, different somehow. Will took a deep breath and stood stiffly. His body reminded him that all was not well.

From behind, a hard blow hit the side of Will's head, blinding him in one eye. He staggered and clutched his walking wand. Another blow struck one of his arms. Will heard bones crack. He screamed. The arm hung uselessly by his side. Sweat poured agonizingly into his one good eye, as he clung to the last vestiges of consciousness and hope. Looking up, it seemed to him that the sorcerer had never looked so large, so all-encompassing of the space around him.

In the stillness of the mountainside, Will and Neves On faced one another.

Fresh, clean air tapped Will's face. Its sharpness kept him from fainting. Powerful moments, riddled with threatening portent, trickled slowly by. Will knew that he was done for, but he also knew something else. Old had told him, and so had Hope.

It was time. It was his time. It was time to be brave. It was time to face his fear. It was time to honour his truth.

Above them, flying high over the entrance to Old's caves, an eagle screeched, loud and clear.

With one arm broken and dangling by his side and one eye blinded, Will looked at Neves On and grinned frighteningly through broken cracked lips that had seen no food for too long. Light-headed, and eager to do what was right at last, Will chuckled and then began to laugh.

It was time to finish what he had started!

CHAPTER 29

Keep your word, speak your truth, Shift your shape and embrace what's new

Bibs stirred and yawned. It was warm inside the cheery golden room, perhaps too warm for a snail. Sleepily, he slid to the bowl on the floor and had a long drink. Refreshed, he looked around. The fire had almost gone out. Strangely, the coals that should have been burned looked completely untouched, as if there had been no fire at all. Bibs shrugged. It was obviously one more of Old's tricks. He slid around and came to rest by two words etched into the floor.

The formula.

The formula to what, he wondered? And where was it? Was it hidden under the words written there? Was it somewhere else? Bibs shook his head. It occurred to him that somewhere in this room there was important information, perhaps a secret only Old had known. He sighed. The great doings of First Ones and unicorns were beyond him. Other words etched in the floor lit fleetingly, and then the last ember in the fire went out. Bibs didn't understand any of it. Soon he dozed, slept, and finally snored.

Bibs dreamed that there was smoke, and that eagles flew and unicorns soared. He dreamed that Hope and Oobaat came to him and smiled. He dreamed that little Bobs was safe in the forest. He dreamed that Rielle and Pud stood on a hilltop and that Pud gazed with human eyes and was much older than any dog had a right to be. Rielle was holding out a hand, calling something. A hood covered much of her face, but he could see that she smiled. Then Bibs heard someone running, but he did not see whom.

Bibs awoke with a start. He had never dreamed before, or at least he did not remember having done so. He wished with all of his snail's heart, that one day he would find the others. Thinking fondly of his friends, he fell fast asleep again.

…

Rana, Hoot and Bobs chatted by the wishing pond. Abruptly, the Tree of Life began to heave, the Ritual of Return billowing from its branches.

'What is it?' Rana whispered.

Silently, Hoot flew to the tallest tree. He waited there for a long time until the Tree of Life settled. Then he flew to join the others.

'What was it?' Rana urged fearfully.

The three friends watched as things were restored and the white mist wafted gently.

'Nothing will ever be the same again,' Hoot finally breathed, 'and soon, my friends, we will know what it means.'

…

The Tower of Dreams sent messages of whispered urgency through its corridors, like veins of information that coursed full of life's blood, energy, and vital knowing.

In Hope's room, Far heard the whispers. Long years of being with Hope made it possible to understand them. Folding her wings with resolve and quiet dignity, she sat on an ancient book and prepared to wait.

Outside, Flightlord was jolted from his snoring slumber. He jumped to his feet and looked around, as if he had been gone for a very long time. Nothing stirred the moat, the almond orchard hummed with bees, and the mud on Hope's window sills barely simmered.

Peeking inside Hope's windows, he saw the butterfly in her contemplation. Seeing clearly from his reflection that he was now completely purple, Flightlord sighed and rolled his eyes. He was alive and well, and there were things to tell his own kind.

With a last quick glance at the butterfly, he forgot about his colour. Within moments, he was flying. The world of dragon was a place of its own. Flightlord took a long look at Wish, and was gone.

...

Rielle stepped toward the crow. Benny did not let her go alone. Together, they faced the bird. With a calm knowing eye, the crow hopped closer.

Hope looked intently at Oobaat. They both glanced at Candela and Coraggio. The herd stood alert with ears pricked, but none of them moved. Little Bobs shivered uncontrollably with fear and exhaustion, but Candela nudged him gently and murmured something in his ear. Nodding, little Bobs sat still.

'Who are you?' Rielle whispered. The whisper seemed to shimmer on the air and resonate around them.

'I am many things, *Rielle*,' the crow responded.

Urgency slapped the wind. Somewhere on the mountain, the Sorcerer of Great Contempt stalked and hunted them. Will and Pud might be in grave danger, yet in a terrible paradox, nothing could now be rushed.

As if reading their minds, the crow shook its head. 'No,' it stated, 'no, I am not Number Seven of the First Ones.'

It paused and then peered up at Rielle questioningly.

'Don't you know me... *Rielle*?'

Confusing thoughts rustled Rielle's mind. *She remembered something*. She took a deep, shuddering breath. Once - it seemed so long ago - she had lived a usual life, in a usual way, in a house with a garden and a friend next door. She had left that life and gone searching for all the best of reasons, and had become lost doing so. Then, in one life-changing moment, Pud had found a unicorn. She looked beside her at Benny. As if he knew her mind, Benny gazed back and nodded. Rielle felt her star-scar grow warm. She looked at the crow. The huge black bird watched and waited patiently, as if there were no urgent moments to attend to beyond that very instant.

Rielle's memories and thoughts rushed her, crowding one after the other.

She had never returned to her old life and nothing had been usual ever again.

A shaft of sunlight that seemed to have gone astray

touched the ground before her, and Rielle remembered another moment when the light had changed, when she had first seen Benny in the forest. She took a deep breath and looked the crow in the eyes.

'You are my past, my present and my future,' she breathed, hardly knowing what she meant.

The crow blinked.

Rielle went on. 'You dwell beyond time and space, and yet you force my memory to see who I was, while you track me in my present, and tell me of things to come.'

The crow waited silently.

Rielle's star-scar tingled as if it brought the message home.

'You reveal when there will be change; you warn me when I am in danger. You travel beside me, in a world that is part darkness, part light, partly here and partly another place.' Rielle paused and shut her eyes, and felt as if all the answers of the ages were flowing through her mind. She opened her eyes again and nodded, as if she and the crow had decided on something together.

'You link me with the father and mother I never did find. You bind me to the earth, you give me foresight, and you fill me with my future power. You make me see with integrity and truth what I need to know. You show me how to embrace the things I must accept. You send me messages from mysterious realms that I still do not fully understand. You push me to seek my dreams and to fulfil a destiny that is mine.' She stopped speaking and in that moment she felt as if she had been born, once more.

The crow peered shrewdly at her. 'You don't need me

anymore, Rielle,' it sighed. 'You will not need me now, and you shall soon see how.' The bird turned to fly away, glanced back and then vanished, as if it had never been.

'*Rielle...* ' it whispered once more, into the wind.

Rielle felt a jolt of reckoning. The voice was gone! She would not have it to guide her anymore. She glanced at Benny and then turned to look at the others. She felt a flicker of uncertainty at the loss. Without realising it, she had come to depend on the voice and its warning call.

In that very moment, a picture flashed vividly inside her mind.

There was a wall built of stone and rock, well tended and cared for. Pud lay beside it. Nearby, holding a white wand, there stood a dark shadow.

In front of the entrance to Old's caves, Will barely stood, or at least she thought it was Will. The young man she saw had blood streaming down his face and his body was broken.

Rielle gasped.

Only the Wand of Time kept Will standing, as his weight pressed into the wood so hard that it moulded a groove in the dirt.

Rielle despaired.

Will was laughing as he faced the sorcerer; he was laughing as if there was nothing to fear.

Rielle looked up. All eyes watched her.

'To the Serpent's Way!' she called, as if she had always commanded unicorns and First Ones.

With a thought, the unicorns and First Ones sent them there.

CHAPTER 30

And I must finish what it is I started

Will laughed until his sides hurt and he no longer knew whether the tears on his face were from pain or mirth. *He had nothing left to lose!* He would fight to the death to keep evil from getting its hands on Old's gold; on eternal life! If there were nothing left to lose, then, surely, he could try anything he wanted now. It was time to find out what this walking wand that Old had given him could do.

Reckless beyond anything he ever thought he could be, and without so much as a tremor in his once fearful heart, Will prepared. This was the third time he would use the wand. He knew what to do.

Taking a deep breath into his scorching lungs, Will sought the words that he would need. From a source greater than him, power unravelled like an uncoiling snake, power that was long unused. He felt the quickening.

Neves On leered, unconcerned. There was no need for him to fear the crippled, damaged human before him, but it was good to gloat and bide his time. He needed Will to do his dirty work; let the human grovel for a while then beg to be healed. Cruelly, he grinned at Will's pathetic attempts to stand.

Beyond pain, and with no time to lose, Will raised the Wand of Time.

'Reparation!' Will called. 'Have back all the damage you have caused! Have it back by ten times three!'

Standing smugly, assured of complete victory and certainly not fearing the broken, blinded Will, Neves On recoiled and staggered. Instinctively, he raised the white wand to fight back, but she bit him with an agonising burn that was so painful he dropped her. Gasping, he was unable to speak.

The full power from the Wand of Time linked, entwined and bound unalterably with the words that Will had just spoken. The force smashed a hole into the side of the mountain and overwhelmed Neves On with an irreversible stunning might. Number Seven of the First Ones was blown pitilessly off his feet and thrown into the air like a rag.

Against the wall of the Serpent's Way, Pud leapt, airborne, freed from the sorcerer's agonising spell. Glancing at Will, the dog ran to escape the madness that erupted.

Smoke and fire mingled with wild winds to flay the mountainside. Will coughed and gasped, new tears coursing down his face. This time, however, they were caused by the sting of corruption meeting itself. From the depths of that corruption, Will and Pud could hear Neves On's screams.

Something beyond them all was doing its work.

Will gasped. Could it be that he had managed to strike evil down? After all his struggles and all his reluctance to try, could it be that he had done it? Could it be so simple? But his broken bones and blinded eye reminded him that there was nothing simple in this moment; that the journey had been long and arduous, and that the fight had begun a very long time ago.

Will gazed at the wand he held. She glowed fully at her centre as she waited for his command. He would never have guessed how much power he held! As if Old were there with them in that moment, the words Old had once spoken to Will boomed in his mind.

Things you make they cannot break
When you hold the Wand of Time!

For a fleeting moment, Will doubted himself again. He doubted the power of his thoughts. How was it possible that someone like him could hope to fight Neves On? Was it even right? Was he capable of wielding the walking wand to only do good, or would he too, one day, be tempted to beckon evil with his new power? Was it wrong, what he had asked for? He knew he had been fighting for his life and he knew that the sorcerer was evil beyond compare, but was it right that he should be the one to make justice happen? What place had he to uphold the laws of right and wrong? He was just an ordinary human. Did he have a right to do this thing?

Will tried to wipe the sweat and tears from his good

eye but he only made it worse. The eye stung with the added mixture of grime and dirt. The effort to breathe, and to keep his mind clear, was bearing down on him. Will suspected he might also be done for, here alone on this mountaintop, with just a dog and a wand to see him through, at the end.

And then, as if the power of the wand could make his deepest desires come true, Will knew he was no longer alone. Silently, as always, the herd and the First Ones wrapped their numbers about him in a wall of protection. Will's heart leapt. He tried to smile. Through the haze of smoke, he saw that Rielle was with them. The sight of them all lit Will's heart with something so true and good and renewing that he almost forgot he was a mere shadow of himself, broken and bleeding beyond recognition. In their timely arrival, the smoke, fire and dark clouds lifted.

With disbelief, all eyes turned to where Neves On lay; frail, weak, apparently broken. The Staff of the Unimaginable rested nearby. The sorcerer looked up at Will. Surprise raged in his eyes. Will almost felt sorry for him but Coraggio caught the thought.

'No, Will,' he called, 'do not stop for pity!'

The sorcerer laughed from deep down in his chest; it was an ugly sound, as usual. 'You were always a weak-willed creature, Will,' he panted. 'Even at the last, you pause for pity.' He tried to laugh again, but the sound gurgled in his throat.

'I, too, stopped for pity once,' Neves On sneered, 'when I was young and wielded another wand.' His breath came harshly with a memory. 'The Wand of Mercy,' he whispered, his face fleetingly sad. The moment passed. 'An inferior wand,' he snarled. He choked with a gasp.

Benny stepped from the herd, looking pointedly at the sorcerer.

'Apologise,' he whispered piercingly, 'do something for yourself. It is not too late to turn it all around.'

Everyone held their breath. The way of unicorns might win yet. Perhaps deep down, deep in his heart, Neves On might realise that all was not lost.

The Sorcerer of Great Contempt raised himself on one elbow. He glanced at Benny and the herd and his gaze lingered on Candela in all her glory. For one moment, just one moment, the way of unicorns did win. Beyond the wildest hopes of all who watched, the sorcerer softened, yielded, began to reach out, then, quickly, frantically, his eyes shut down.

'Never!' he spat. 'Never! It's too late for me!'

Will felt the presence of Old, then, as if Old were there beside him. He raised the Wand of Time, even though the action tore harshly at his wounds. He gasped from the effort.

'It's not too late,' Will breathed. 'Old showed me that. It's never too late to change how you've been.'

In a lightning move, despite his injuries, the sorcerer leapt to his feet. 'It's too late!' he shrieked. 'There's no going back for someone like me!' Then, with every ounce of strength and wit and power left within him, he sent a huge ball of fire to the unicorn herd.

The world slowed. Everything slowed. Rielle watched

as birds flew and trees swayed, unhurriedly. She watched, helpless, as Will stepped in front of the molten fire. As if in a vision, she could have sworn that Old stood by Will! The vision of Old said something to him. Rielle gasped. A memory of Old handing the wand to Will came swiftly to her mind's eye.

Things you make, they cannot break, when you hold the Wand of Time!

There was nothing else that could be done now. It was time to make the unbreakable decision, time for Will to finish what he'd started.

Despite his broken arm and blind eye, Will stood as tall as he'd ever done. His eyes shone as Rielle had never seen them shine, and for the first time since he could remember, Will felt truly alive. He was looking death in the eye now. But he had made his decision and it was time to live!

Will brandished the Wand of Time and called the words-of-no-return, shouting them as if he had always known them; they were words that time would never break.

Neves On, be gone, be gone!
Neves On, your day is done!
Neves On, justice waits
Neves On, you choose your fate!
Spirit, Fire, Air, Earth, Water
Moon, stars, sun and sky
I call out with the Wand of Time
And send you back to before life began!

Darkness erupted on the mountain. It filled the sight of every living thing that watched, for miles around. Such darkness, that the unicorns felt the Ritual of Return dim. They restored it in less than a heartbeat.

Rielle felt faint with sickness. A cold nose pressed into her hand. Falling to her knees, she clasped Pud hard. He licked her ears and face with such conviction that despite the eruption around them, Rielle almost smiled. Little Bobs squealed so loudly that Hope felt compelled to hunker down and take him in his hands. Oobaat held the Staff of Life high, muttering words only known to First Ones.

From the madness, Neves On screamed. 'I'll change! I'll change. I can do it now, just let me try! I wasn't sure before! I wasn't sure before… I can do it now! I can do it now!'

His begging and pleading struck at the hearts of those who stood there, but Will's words were spoken; it was too late for him to change his mind. Then the wildness roared so loudly in their ears they could no longer hear anything.

Will stood, transfixed. He was still alive. He had faced death and his fears! Neither the darkness nor the madness nor the horror around them could touch him. He was no longer afraid. He clung to the Wand of Time as she pulsed with the power he had just created. Thoughts raced through his mind.

What would happen next? Was this black, stinking, roaring catastrophe ever going to end? What would be on the other side? Would they all still be the same?

Beside him, he felt the presence of Old, as if it were Old that kept him standing tall. Old seemed to whisper to Will.

'You can finish it now.'

Surprised, Will realised that he still held the power of the moment; that he could call away the roaring destruction, as swiftly as he had asked for it.

'Enough!' Will cried, as if calling to the elements was his usual task.

The noise, the darkness and the stench cleared slowly, hesitantly, as if reluctant to reveal what remained on the mountainside.

Rielle stood, her hand still placed on Pud's head. Hope made sure that little Bobs was alright and he, too, stood. Oobaat lowered his wand and waited. Each member of the unicorn herd touched horns to the unicorn standing beside them.

Will stood like a warrior, tall, upright, his eyes blazing as if he had seen something beyond him. The Wand of Time glowed golden in her centre. At last, she had performed her greatest task. The Sorcerer of Great Contempt, Neves On, Number Seven of the First Ones, was no more. In his place there stood a large boulder of plain grey stone.

The mountain grunted then became still.

It was over.

As if reminding him of his humanity after all, Will collapsed and fell to his knees. The Wand of Time lay quietly by him. Will's frail body shuddered with relief. It was not easy to do justice. It was not easy to do the bidding of the Oath of Law. He flinched in his mind at what could have been. But the sorcerer had not won.

'Now there are only two First Ones left,' Will sobbed.

Rielle went to him and gently took his unbroken hand. 'He had to be overcome,' she whispered, 'it was he who pushed you, not you him. Old would be so proud… so proud. You finished what you started, Will.'

The herd waited with heads bowed, like a wall of iridescent strength. Little Bobs hung his head, not in sorrow but in relief. Pud watched on with understanding too great for a dog; he too had held a walking wand, the Wand of Time, no less. Pud looked up at Rielle and his amber eyes showed that he would never be the same dog again.

Inside the mountain, in Old's room, Bibs sharply awoke. He had just had the most wonderful dream; something that he would never forget!

CHAPTER 31

Not in big... but in little things

Cautiously, with something like sadness, Oobaat walked to the rock.

'Goodbye,' he whispered, 'goodbye. I'll think of how you were when we were young and you were still merciful.'

Stooping, Oobaat picked up the Staff of the Unimaginable. He was moved to shed a tear by what he saw. 'You're safe,' he murmured, 'you're safe at last.' And then, gently, where the wand was not burned or cut, he held her. The wand lay in his hands, voiceless and ruined. 'Please,' Oobaat begged, 'the world needs you to live!'

Suddenly, there was singing. It was the Wand of Faith.

Oobaat chuckled and looked at Hope. 'Thank you brother,' he whispered, 'thank you.'

Hope shook his head, puzzled. 'I did nothing,' he replied, as he watched the Wand of Faith glow from within, 'she sang on her own.'

Then, as if they too had to try, the Wand of Time and the Staff of Life joined their voices to the song. All three voices soared.

Rielle couldn't bear it. She thought her heart would break.

'Live,' cried Oobaat to the Staff of the Unimaginable, 'live, please live! The others sing for you, don't you see?'

The wand lay still. Too many cuts and burns bruised her white wood.

The unicorn herd kneeled as one. Touching their horns to the ground, they chanted softly, magnificently.

From time begun
When thought was new
Lilifel and First Ones
Together grew

All knowing, all powerful
All seeing
All strong
So it was life begun

With power earned
Of truth, of love
Lilifel's call justice
To heal the white one

Spirit, Fire, Air, Earth and Water
Moon, Stars, Sun and Sky
With the Wands of Light
All tasks are not done

Give back the wand of all imagining
Give back the wand of all law

Give back the wand of all knowing
Give back the wand of Unicorn.

The herd stood. Candela nodded to Benny and Benny went to Oobaat.

With understanding in his tired, wise face, Oobaat held the Staff of the Unimaginable like an offering, in both hands. Benny shut his eyes. When he opened them, his horn glowed golden. Gently, he lowered his horn to touch the wand. Oobaat gasped. A shock of power that even he didn't expect coursed through her.

Benny stepped back. 'Soon,' Benny spoke to Oobaat, in a light, clear voice, 'soon you will return to your pond and, if you choose, become a tortoise again. But now, just one more time, Number One of the First Ones, Eno On, just one more time... for this wand made by Unicorn from the Tree of Life, this one wand that grants all that is true, just one more time, ask for her to live again.'

Oobaat nodded. It was true. The Staff of the Unimaginable was the first wand, born from a limb of the Tree of Life and made by unicorns. The most powerful wand of all! How she must have suffered in the sorcerer's evil hands. Made with love, goodness and truth, she had been forced into evil, fear and misuse. Neves On had turned his back on so much good. He had used this most treasured of all wands to warp and taint what was right. Renewed by Benny's power, Oobaat brushed the wand one more time.

Like a fresh spring morning when all things are clean,

before memory and life make things too hard, the Staff of the Unimaginable began to sing!

Destiny is in our keeping
Tomorrow there will be no weeping
All things are done
Unicorns and the One

Spirit, Fire, Air, Earth and Water
Moon, Stars, Sun and Sky
All things are done
Unicorns, mortals and First Ones arrive.

'Look!' called Rielle, pointing to the rock.

As the wand sang, the rock began to vanish. Louder the wand sang, until its voice filled the mountain, the valleys, the sky and the heavens. As it did so, they watched the rock shrink and then dissolve into nothing.

At last the wand stopped singing; she was almost healed. Just five deep cuts and burns remained, the ones made that fateful day in the battle of the almond orchard. It was as if they were a testament to Old.

Holding her in both hands, Oobaat turned to the herd.

'Can she ever be mended?' he asked. 'Can she ever be whole?'

Candela stepped forward. 'Carry her for us as you have done before,' she implored, 'be her bearer for us once again.' She paused. 'Take her back to the forest where the Tree of Life will tell us how to make her whole.'

Oobaat faltered. 'I let you down, remember,' he

murmured. 'I lost her when you had faith in me to keep her safe.'

Candela smiled. 'Mistakes we make once are our teachers,' she replied, 'and something tells me you would not lose her again.'

Coraggio stepped forward. 'We must find Bibs,' he announced, 'and then it will be time for us to return to the forest.'

The herd trilled in joyful reply.

Wearily, Will tried to stand. Hope hurried to his side.

'Wait,' Hope cautioned, 'wait. There is no need for a hero to rush.' He smiled down at Will as he and Oobaat coursed blue light from their wands onto him, as the unicorn herd poured their white light.

'You will heal.' Hope smiled. 'There's no need to worry about that.' He hesitated. 'But I'm afraid that in your damaged eye, you will always be blind. For some reason I do not understand, it will never see again.' It was unusual for a mix of blue and white light not to heal. 'The damage is too great,' Hope explained.

Will nodded. The expression on his face showed that he always knew there would be a price to pay.

Rielle turned to Will. 'Wait!' she cried, rummaging in her travel sack. 'Here,' she smiled at him, 'here,' and in her hand she held out to him, a piece of black cloth.

'Old's eye patch!' Will exclaimed.

Rielle nodded. 'I've kept it with me always,' she whispered. 'I couldn't bear to let it go.'

Will's good eye became moist. He thought his heart would break.

'Put it on for him,' Hope urged, 'he needs you to help him, Rielle.'

Carefully, Rielle placed the eye patch over Will's poor, blinded eye, making sure it was snug.

'You have Old's wand, and you've been inside his mountain... it seems only right that you should have this too. Old treasured them all.' Rielle paused, almost shyly. 'I have something else for you.'

From beneath her cloak, she pulled out Will's ridiculous hat. It was terribly crushed and looked even sillier than before, but proudly, she held it out.

Will chuckled softly and his heart squeezed. He was still weak from the effort of it all, yet here stood Rielle, fussing over small, wonderful things.

Will looked at Candela and she nodded. In that moment, he wanted to ask Rielle about the riddle and truth of unicorns.

Gratefully, Will stood, stumbling a little. Rielle took his arm. He paused and looked at her as if he'd never truly seen her before. It was as if now, with only one eye, he saw what he used to miss.

'What?' Rielle asked, embarrassed by his stare.

'You are a true, dear, cherished friend to me,' Will smiled.

Rielle blushed. 'All I know is that I'll hit you if you ever try to get yourself killed again!' Overcome with emotion, she let Will lean on her harder as she pretended to look ahead. She nudged Pud and grinned. Pud nudged her back then sneezed a huge, happy sneeze.

The unicorn herd walked behind, overjoyed. Finally, the task was over. Their beloved forest beckoned!

Coraggio stepped up to Will and looked carefully at him. 'We're all proud of you Will, you must know that.' He smiled. 'You've proven yourself to be a true warrior who fights with a kind and loving heart, and only when he must.'

Will stopped walking. All eyes were on him: Benny, little Bobs, the herd, the First Ones, Rielle and Pud. Such faithful and wonderful friends, all of them! Will felt undeserving, but just as he had the thought, he remembered something the wand had sung.

In the end, the challenge lies for all of us
Not in big, but in little things.

Will caught his breath. 'Before I ever went to Wish all that time ago, I wished and wanted to make my father proud.'

He paused, exhausted, and leaned into Rielle. She took the extra weight until he could stand.

Will continued. 'My father was indeed a king, but I was the youngest son and the eleventh child. No one ever called me prince, so I told it to myself. As for being a warrior, well, that was just a lie.' He nodded regretfully. 'I thought that if I did something that my brothers had not, then I could win my father's love and be better than the rest of them.' Regret scavenged his face.

'And so it was, my friends, that with my father's stolen gold, my brother's fine hat, and a manner I thought was clever and bold, I chose to make a wish. I wished and wished. Then, one day, I charged the shores of Wish itself. The wish I made is now well known. In my ignorance and pride, the wish I chose was to slay a unicorn for the precious horn.'

Will bowed his head.

'The wish I made that day led me here today.' He took a deep breath. 'I could have wished for anything, but that is what I chose.' Will sighed and nodded. 'A regrettable day? Yes, in many ways, but who would have thought that my wish would finally come true in other ways, ways that I never thought of? Yes, I have become a warrior, but at a price! I have become proud to say my name, but only after a long, winding and painful road. I could now look in a mirror and not want to run in shame. I have made friends beyond compare, found that truth is always what counts, but to any and all that would make a wish, I have this to say.' Will paused and caught his breath.

The unicorn herd stood at attention, their eyes pinned on him. Hope and Oobaat with their good, trustworthy faces peered at him with sharp, wise eyes. Little Bobs and Pud looked up at him as if his words were made of gold, and Rielle, dear Rielle, stood beside him, like a solid wall.

Will sighed. 'I would say one thing to those who make their wishes, and it is only this. Be careful what you wish for and do so with a careful heart. Nothing worth having is ever easy, and truth is the only road.'

CHAPTER 32

Simply Hope

Beyond the mountain's view, the sun had sunk into a finite skyline. Its last orange rays waved goodbye.

Just as the group began to breathe freely again, a careering figure bolted from inside the mountain, crashing and rolling into the Serpent's Way. Everyone gaped.

'Bibs!' bellowed little Bobs.

Bibs righted himself. 'I've been in *there!*' he called, goggle eyed. 'I found Old's room... an eagle carried me... I made a fire... I got stuck... I read a rhyme... and I finally got tired of waiting and found a way to get out!' He looked around at the astonished faces. 'Has much been happening?' he asked.

With a roar of irony, the group laughed until they could laugh no more. Bibs wasn't sure what they were laughing at, but red cheeked, he joined in.

'Alright,' Coraggio finally gasped, 'it's time to go back to the forest, my friends.'

'Wait,' Hope exclaimed, 'wait!'

Everyone standing on the ridge looked at Hope with eyes full of the past few months, filled with memories and events.

Hope turned to Rielle. In a swift movement, he held the Wand of Faith in both hands and gestured that she should take it.

Rielle blinked and frowned at him.

'Take her!' Hope commanded.

Rielle wavered. 'But....' she began.

Hope scowled fiercely as if any moment he might regret his choice, his voice filled with emotion.

'Take the Wand of Faith, Rielle, and make your dream come true! That's what you've been searching for, isn't it? Your dream!'

Rielle stared at the wand. 'Yes,' she replied cautiously, 'you know it is. Of course I've been searching for my dream, but....'

'No,' Hope growled, glancing at Will, 'no, you cannot refuse. You have no more choice in the matter than Will did when he was handed the Wand of Time. Now take her.'

Will watched, bemused, the Wand of Time held casually in his hand as if she were a simple walking cane.

Rielle looked at the herd. Benny winked and grinned. Oobaat nodded kindly and the herd trilled softly.

She reached out to take the wand - *Hope's wand*. As her first fingers touched her, the wand began to hum. Rielle almost recoiled at the touch. She held the wand at arm's length as power surged into her arms and through her body like a thirsty mountain stream.

Hope stood back and watched her.

Rielle became breathless and her throat squeezed. Quickly, she looked at Will. He smiled as if he understood her in that moment, better than anyone there. Rielle blinked. The Wand of Faith shone softly at her core, her dark brown wood aglow.

'You know what this means, don't you, Rielle?' Candela whispered into the new dark of night.

'I… I'm not sure,' Rielle replied. A part of her wanted to hand the wand back, while a part of her was honoured by the gesture.

Perhaps her dream was too big for her? She was, after all, just an ordinary girl.

But in that moment, she watched Oobaat hand the Staff of the Unimaginable to Hope. Number Nine of the First Ones, Enin On, held the unicorn wand now, and somehow it all felt right. For a fleeting moment, the unicorn horns glowed golden, as the Ritual of Return encompassed him.

Enin On turned to Rielle and his look told her that this was a place of no return. He and Rielle smiled at each other, as if the Wand of Faith gave them something only they could share.

'Does this mean you won't be going back to the Tower of Dreams?' Rielle asked, hesitantly.

'That's right,' Enin On replied.

Rielle took a deep breath. 'But what about Far and your room full of books and potions and… and the sixteenth door and all the things you'd be leaving behind?'

Enin On chuckled. 'Do you really need to ask?' he replied, with a twinkle in his eye. 'Oh, and while I think of it, you need one more thing to make this complete.'

Calmly, Number Nine of the First Ones removed the hood from his head and took his brown cloak off, placing it carefully over Rielle's own. 'I shall fashion myself a new cloak,' he stated. 'Hope's cloak is now yours.'

Rielle looked shyly at Will and the herd. Once again, Benny winked at her. Pud nudged her so hard she clutched the wand for balance.

The Wand of Faith took her cue:

From wishes, from wishes
Come all your desires
From desires
Come all your dreams

From dreams, from dreams
Come all your hopes
From hopes
Come your schemes, and your plans

Be brave, be brave
Don't hide or hold back
Endeavour
And you will aspire

Believe, believe
Trust in yourself
Let your heart and your mind
Conspire

From wishes, from wishes
Come all your dreams
And from dreams come
Your wisdom and power.

The wand stopped singing but continued to glow.

'So you've given me your... er... job?' Rielle whispered, amazed.

Grinning broadly, Enin On placed a comforting hand on her shoulder.

'My place in the Tower of Dreams is now yours, Rielle, and everything that goes with it.'

'What will *you* do now, though?' Rielle asked with a surge of timid excitement.

Enin On turned and faced the herd. 'I will guard the Staff of the Unimaginable and go to wherever that takes me.' He held the unicorn wand carefully. 'She needs to be repaired and to have the missing pieces of her knowledge restored. That could take a very long time.' He paused.

'Remember, this was the first wand, and my job will now be a long one. I will no longer have time to be *Hope*.' He touched the white wand carefully. Her charred scores looked dull. 'Who knows where it will lead me?' He looked kindly at Rielle. 'You are fit to follow your dream, Rielle. You have shown it in many ways.'

'I'm not a First One, though,' Rielle questioned.

Will stepped forward. 'I was no First One,' he smiled, 'but it didn't stop Old giving me this.' He grinned as he flourished the walking wand. 'Nothing stands still, Rielle, that's what I know now. You can do it! We were both handed our wands for a reason.'

Rielle nodded.

'Besides,' Will went on, 'it means we can visit each other this way, as quickly as a thought.'

Rielle looked surprised. 'Aren't you going home,

then?' she asked, embarrassed to sound so pleased.

Will shook his head. Sheepishly, he looked at the others.

'No,' he chuckled, 'after all the fuss I've made. But no, I still have so much to do and learn, and I've come to like Old's mountain.'

Candela smiled. 'I think they're your caves and it is your mountain now, Will,' she reassured. 'Eerht ytnewt On would expect you to think that. You have earned the privilege.'

'Nonetheless,' Will murmured, looking wistfully around, 'nonetheless, I will keep calling this Old's mountain.'

He and Rielle smiled at each other.

'You become more like him all the time,' Rielle laughed.

Will beamed. 'Good,' he grinned, before becoming serious again. 'Remember what Old said to me, that morning long ago, in the almond orchard when he lay... dying.' He lowered his voice to a hush. 'For the longest time I would not believe.'

Rielle nodded. She whispered the words. '*You are as I was, and I am as you will be.*' Her eyes moistened. 'That's what he said to you, Will.' She and Will looked quietly at each other, sharing a private bond.

'I'm staying with you!' Bibs unexpectedly called, looking up at Will.

'Me?' Will gasped. 'You want to stay with me? Here in Old's caves?'

'Yes,' Bibs muttered, 'after all, it's the least I can do. That old eagle did put me here for a reason, and I've decided that it would be good for me.'

Pud barked and pushed Bibs over with his nose.

The herd chuckled. 'We will make sure that little Bobs arrives safely home then,' Coraggio said, 'and now, we must go!'

'Wait,' cried Rielle, 'what about Old's gold? It's here somewhere. What happens to that now?'

Coraggio chuckled. 'That is precisely the point, Rielle. It is Old's gold, not ours. Old's knowledge. Not ours.' He looked at the entrance to Old's caves. 'We only wanted to find it so that we could protect it from evil. Now we will leave it alone.'

Benny trotted up to Rielle. 'I will visit you often in the Tower of Dreams,' he assured. 'You haven't seen the last of me.'

Rielle hugged him hard. 'You,' she smiled, 'if it wasn't for you, my dearest Benny, I would never have known I even *had* a dream. It's because of you that wonderful things have happened for me.'

Benny grinned.

Candela stepped forward. 'Is it?' she asked. 'Or were we all just playing into destiny's hand?'

The words were barely out of her mouth when the four wands began to sing.

The truth of time
We have been seeking
Destiny
We are now meeting
Mastery is not in keeping
It comes not from hands
But from hearts

It comes from knowing
Understanding
At last.

Above them, an eagle called, and then swiftly, it was gone. The Ritual of Return was flowing heavily from the herd. 'It is time!' Coraggio called.

A last look passed from Will and Rielle to the First Ones, the herd and little Bobs, and then, with a thought, the unicorns and the others were gone.

The only thing that lit the steadfast night were the stars above and the light at the core of the two wands handed from First Ones to humans.

Will and Rielle faced each other, knowing it was now their charge to carry on, with courage and conviction, the tasks that had been begun for them.

Will reached out and took Rielle's right hand in his left one. Rielle noticed that his hand was softer than doe hair and twice as smooth. She felt as if her heart would burst. For long minutes they watched the sky. Pinpricks of light filtered through the black blanket as the stars seemed to speak to them.

'Remember,' Will said, 'we have our wands. We can visit each other with just a thought.'

Rielle squeezed his hand. 'We have a lot to learn about our new lives, haven't we?' she breathed.

'Yes,' Will sighed, 'but we shan't be alone. We will have each other, and the First Ones and the unicorns will always be there for us, if we need them.'

Again Rielle squeezed his hand. 'I suppose I should

go and break the news to Far,' she giggled.

Will smiled. He suddenly remembered her as the girl who had crashed into him in the orchard on that fateful day, when both their worlds would never be the same again. How they had argued with each other at first, only to discover that they would be fond friends.

The mountain rumbled briefly and ice winds whipped them.

Will and Rielle hugged with a moment of sweetness in their happy hearts.

Rielle gathered her thoughts about her. Already she could feel the tug of the Tower. 'I will go now,' she whispered, her heart in her throat. 'The Tower of Dreams has been missing Hope for too long.'

She stepped back. 'Come, faithful Pud, it's time I went to begin my dream.' With an almost shy smile at Will, she touched the Wand of Faith on the ground, and was gone.

Will grinned wistfully. Without realising it, he smoothed his eye patch then ran his thumb over the whittled eagle in his pocket.

'Well Bibs,' he said matter-of-factly, 'there are places here inside Old's mountain that a man has yet to discover. And I think it's time to fill you in on the things that happened while you were snugly waiting for us all.' He cocked an eyebrow at the snail. 'Are you game?'

Bibs chuckled. 'Let me show you Old's caves,' he replied.

...

It was a soft, summery early morning in Wish. Sunshine drifted longingly through the windows of Hope's room and Far dozed on a pile of books.

Rielle stood quietly in the centre of the room that she barely knew, yet she felt as if she were coming home. She looked around with excitement and joy, and something more that she couldn't describe. There was so much to learn! Emotion welled in her eyes. She smiled almost ruefully. The Tower of Dreams! Who would ever have thought she would return, let alone make it her home?

Far awoke. 'Rielle,' she roared, 'I've missed you so!'

Rielle nodded, her eyes aglow. In a gentle motion she pulled the plain brown hood from her head.

'Call me Hope,' she breathed, 'just Hope, simply Hope.'

Pud looked up at her with his amber eyes, then sighed and placed a giant paw onto her shoe.

'Well,' Far beamed, 'I knew I would be there when you found your dream.'

Just then, the Wand of Faith began to sing a brand new song.

♦♦♦♦♦♦♦♦♦

'Nothing ever ends'

The Unicorns of Wish Books

WISH

WISH AGAIN

THE THIRD WISH

HOPE

JOURNEY OF TREES

About the Author

Deby Adair is a writer and artist. She loves all animals and believes we must take care of our natural world.

UnicornKisses

www.ingramcontent.com/pod-product-compliance
Lightning Source LLC
Chambersburg PA
CBHW030641110726
47901CB00002B/532